WESTERN ISLE

Readers are requested to take great care of the books while in their possession, and to point out any defects that they may notice in them to the Librarian.

This book is issued for a period of twenty-one days and should be returned on or before the latest date stamped below, but an extension of the period of loan may be granted when desired.

DATE OF RETURN	DATE OF RETURN	DATE OF RETURN
. . . .	. . . .	. . . .
. . . .	. . . .	. . . .
. . . .	. . . .	. . . .
. . . .	. . . .	. . . .
. . . .	. . . .	. . . .
. . . .	. . . .	. . . .
. . . .	. . . .	. . . .
. . . .	. . . .	. . . .
. . . .	. . . .	. . . .
. . . .	. . . .	. . . .
. . . .	. . . .	. . . .
. . . .	. . . .	. . . .
. . . .	. . . .	. . . .
. . . .	. . . .	. . . .

THE SKY GREW RED

ANNE HOLM

Translated from Danish
by Patricia Crampton

MAMMOTH

This story is for John

First published in Great Britain 1991
by Methuen Children's Books Ltd
Published 1992 by Mammoth
an imprint of Reed Consumer Books Limited
Michelin House, 81 Fulham Road, London SW3 6RB
and Auckland, Melbourne, Singapore and Toronto
Reprinted 1992 (twice)

ISBN 0 7497 1041 1

A CIP catalogue record for this title
is available from the British Library

Printed in Great Britain by
BPCC Hazells Ltd
Member of BPCC Ltd

Contents

Contents

Foreword

You can read a foreword before you read the story, or when you are in the middle of it. You can also read it afterwards, or you can just skip it altogether!

This foreword is here to tell you that the story of 'the sky grew red' took place nearly two hundred years ago, during the wars against Napoleon. Many things were different in those days. For instance, a clear distinction was made between men and women, and therefore between girls and boys as well. People were divided into groups in a different way, too, not according to how many cars or stereos they owned – none of those things had been invented yet; they were divided up according to the way they spoke, how much they knew, and how they behaved towards other people.

Many things are better nowadays; I think there are also some things that were better then. What is exciting is that behind all the outward things and

7

ways, the people themselves were very much the same as they are now, and so were the children.

Chapter One

Louise looked up at the sky – if Miss Gertrude did not come soon they would not be home before dark and Grandfather would be angry and Miss Gertrude would get upset and wring her hands and explain and explain, because she did not know Grandfather well enough to realise that he only made a fuss because he worried about their driving in the dark.

But it was never really dark here in Denmark in summertime, not as it had been, at home in the West Indies. Here in Denmark the light lingered long after the sun had set – so the darkness was never truly dark.

Louise smiled a little at the thought of her two 'homes': which of them really was her home? Sometimes she felt as if home was no longer anywhere. She got up from the seat; the gardener had told her that there were sure to be ripe raspberries in the orchard.

And he was right. The rhubarb leaf, which she had

fastened with a straw in the shape of a cornet, was soon filled up now. She peered across towards the big white house, but there was still no sign of Miss Gertrude.

Below the tall beech trees further down the slope you could sit and watch the Sound. The seat was quite mossy – oh, well, never mind, her skirt was already spotted with raspberry juice. Louise sighed; here in Denmark there was such a fuss when your clothes got dirty: 'You really must pay more attention', and 'A well brought-up little girl should learn to be clean and tidy', and 'The maids have better things to do than to spend their whole time washing for children'.

At home in St Croix they changed into fresh dresses at least twice a day, but of course, it was much hotter there, so naturally you got creased and sweaty. By now Louise was so absorbed in the raspberries, and in wondering about 'home' that she did not even notice him until he was standing in front of her.

The girl let out a frightened little gasp and looked up at him, her eyes wide. It had been silly of him to come on her so suddenly. After all, girls screamed at the slightest excuse – but the seat down there in the shade had looked so good and he needed to catch his breath for a while. Tim took another look at the girl, sitting there, still as a mouse, just like some little woodland animal thinking it will be invisible if it does not move a muscle. She really had been frightened, it was not just ordinary girlish whimpering: you could not turn pale like that at will.

'Good afternoon,' he said politely. 'May I sit beside you for a little while? I've been on the move all day.'

The girl nodded silently, but her pallor was receding and she was holding out the cornet to him.

'Oh, thanks!' he said. 'I'm Tim. They're good, aren't they?'

'Have some more. My name's Louise.'

Tim nodded.

'The Sound is quiet today even with our ships not far away.'

'Yes,' said Louise gratefully, and Tim looked at her in surprise.

'I'm ... I'm afraid of sailors,' she said, lifting her chin with a defiant look, her blue eyes growing large and dark again. Tim said comfortingly that they would not hurt children. She made a gesture as if to protest, but said only: 'Do you think there really will be war, in this country, I mean?'

Tim thought of all the talk he had heard the night before, at home with Aunt Isabel. 'Yes, I'm afraid so,' he said.

The girl looked gravely at him. 'I can't understand it,' she said. 'I mean, Denmark has not done anything

11

to England, so why can't they simply be allowed to be neu...neutral? That's what I can't understand.'

Tim felt rather as if he were two people: after all, it *was* all very exciting, and the great ships with their sails set were a marvellous sight – and to see a real sea battle! That would be something to talk about at home. Aunt Isabel had been angry last night, in fact she had told Admiral Gambier so to his face: 'It's not fair,' she had said, 'you lie out there, stocking up joints of beef and flour and what have you; if there are any planks and timber to be found, they are bought and hauled on board, without the poor people being told they will be used to land enemy soldiers in their country. I call that making fools of decent folk who are simply looking after their trade. Lord Nelson, all honour to his memory, would never have agreed to that kind of thing!'

Admiral Gambier had listened to her gravely and calmly until she spoke of Lord Nelson; then he had gone red in the face and retorted: 'Lord Nelson obeyed orders and did his duty, as the rest of us must, ma'am.'

But he had not looked enthusiastic.

Tim wondered whether he should try to explain some of this, but he contented himself by saying that other people could not understand it, either. Then he thought that, after all, he ought to say something more: 'You must remember that England is at war;

you can't blame them for thinking what might happen if Denmark let Bonaparte use their ships, can you?'

He never knew what she might have answered, for at that moment someone called to her from the house. 'I must run,' she said hastily. 'We've got quite a way to go before nightfall.' She pushed the rhubarb leaf with the raspberries into his hands and before he could answer she was already no more than a pale flower that fluttered across the park and disappeared.

Louise could not sleep. She *had* slept, and probably for some time, because the whole house was filled with the stillness of night, but she had been dreaming that old dream again, about the ships fighting and burning. Perhaps she could have slept, but she did not dare to. She did not have bad dreams so often these days; it had probably happened because she had been thinking last night about what 'home' really meant to her. Father and Mother and all the rest were so far away, and not just because it was a long, long voyage. Somehow she could not remember them properly, as real people. They were becoming pictures: Father, with his worried look, because he never knew if the ships he sent away filled with goods would arrive where they should, or if they would be taken by the English, and Mother, who was always so busy — 'You children are more than a handful,' as she always said. Now there were only eight in the house over there, while here Grandfather and Uncle Drewsen had a household of ten, including herself. You could not really miss people who had turned into pictures. Except, of course, Dolly, fat, black, happy Dolly, who always had time and a pair of open arms for a hug, a soft, shining cheek to lean against, warm little kisses and gentle, murmuring words — because she did not believe that children should obey but not be cuddled. Once Louise had heard her mother protesting to her father, and her father had said that she should let Dolly do as she wished. 'For Dolly it's natural to show little children that you love them; who knows, maybe she's the one who's right?'

What time was it? Louise crept out of her bed and over to Emily's empty one to look at her clock. Emily must have forgotten it in the rush of leaving. Four o'clock – then it would soon be light.

Louise wrapped her blanket round her and sat on the ledge by the open window. It was wonderful to have the room entirely to herself, and altogether wonderful that only Grandfather and Miss Gertrude were left in the house. All those children, every day from morning to night, were sometimes too much. In fact she liked the little ones very much, but grown-ups always thought that as long as children were the

14

same age they would get on together, so it had been decided as soon as she arrived last year that when all the children from Springforbye were there too, she should share her room with Emily, Uncle Drewsen's half-sister. In any case, Emily was fourteen, two years older than Louise, so perhaps that was what made her a bit silly – very nice, perhaps, but silly, not the sort of person you could really talk to.

Not like him – the boy she had met yesterday up in 'Enrum's' Park. Not that they had talked much: nevertheless, she had the feeling that she *could* have had a real talk with him, he was not at all superior, as boys usually were. It was a pity Miss Gertrude had called her at that very moment; he had sounded so fair, and so steady and unruffled. Louise had never realized before that the English might be afraid of Bonaparte. Suddenly she sat up straight: the English!

They had spoken to each other in English! She had been sitting there, thinking about St Croix and all the family there, and he had said 'Good afternoon!' and she had simply answered in English without thinking about it, because she already had the family over there in her head, and was so used to speaking both languages.

Tim was English! She had been eating raspberries with an English boy, while all the time Uncle Drewsen was in Copenhagen with all the other children and Aunt Philla and Aunt Christine, because he was a first lieutenant in the Militia and might perhaps have to fight the English, if all the rumours were true.

But they could not be true, thought Louise, with relief. The English must realize by now that the Danes had not liked Bonaparte for a long time now. That was why the Crown Prince had left Copenhagen after only two days – not because he didn't care about the city, or didn't know what was going on.

Only Tim had thought that there really would be war. One would think he would know, being an Englishman?

Louise shivered a little in a chill breath of wind from the Sound. Where was he living? Of course there were a lot of English people in Elsinore, merchants and ships' chandlers, some of them rich, like the Danes who lived at Lingby Lakes in summertime, and up here on the coast. Perhaps his father was rich and they had a summer place near Vedbaek?

Grandfather was pretty rich, too, she supposed and so was Uncle Drewsen. But most of all they were very nice; by day they were busy at the mill and up at the farm, but in the evening it was such fun here, when there were guests and they sang and danced and put on tableaux. Mrs Rahbek from Hill House could make the most incredible things, cutting out and gluing flowers and making things up, and Miss

Heger too — well, of course, they were sisters. She was engaged to that young poet with the long German name.

Probably all those grown-ups who had been here so often in the summer, and sung and danced and talked about books and plays and something they called the 'freedom of the press', which they were very keen about — they would all be fighting and going off to war, if it came.

Louise shivered again. How could one go to war with ships? In Copenhagen, that is. What could Uncle Drewsen and the others do in Copenhagen, with a war out on the Sound? If only she had managed to ask Tim a few more questions.

But if there were to be a war, he would become an enemy! And she would become *his* enemy! That is, if he knew she was Danish...

The sky was a brilliant rosy-red now, with borders and beams of gold that were reflected in the peaceful Sound.

Of course there would be no war here. Naturally, one had to fight Bonaparte, since he thought he should own the world; only not here. The Crown Prince had explained to the English ambassador that he would not dream of lending ships to Bonaparte, so England had no need to fear the Danes. Not even grown-ups could think of making war and fighting, when everything was so quiet and peaceful, and the sun was rising in a ring of light, like a song beginning far away.

It was nearly eight when Louise woke up again. Today was 16 August, only four days to Miss Gertrude's birthday. Louise thought regretfully about all their plans to make it really special, to show her that she should not take it too hard when they were naughty. Emily had embroidered a handkerchief for her: 'She'll find that useful to snivel in,' she had said; it had sounded rather unkind, but the handkerchief was pretty – the part of it that was finished, that is, before they all left for the capital. Ophelia had stuck flowers on a box for her, not very like the nice boxes that Mrs Rahbek made, but Ophelia was only six years old and she certainly meant well. Louise herself had written a birthday poem about Fyn, the place where Miss Gertrude's father was the parson. Not that Louise knew what Fyn looked like, but it rhymed very well and when Christian recited it aloud at the breakfast table, with lavish gestures, like Mr Rosing the actor, it would probably have sounded all right.

Only it did not look as if there would be a birthday party now, apart from what she and Grandfather could arrange on their own, for to judge from all the bits and bobs the aunts had taken away with them, they would certainly not be coming home to join in.

Perhaps she should have said she would like to go with them after all? The aunts had changed their minds several times: would it be best for her to be with all the others in town, protected by ramparts and soldiers, or should she stay out here in the fresh air? Yes, because after all it was 'for the sake of her health' that she had been sent to Denmark, as if being a little too easily scared was an illness! But of course, grown-ups simply did not understand.

But Grandfather had looked a little lost when he came down from Springforbye to take over the mill while Uncle Drewsen was in Copenhagen, and that was when she had said she would prefer to stay here at home.

Aunt Philla had probably been quite relieved; they were going to stay with Bartholin, the head gamekeeper, and there really would be a huge crowd of people to take care of.

Louise hurried to wash and dress. Fortunately yesterday's dress was hopelessly dirtied, and since there was no one to stop her, she might just as well wear the white dress with forget-me-nots on it. If only the sash had not been so short — and it was a silly idea to have the waistband right up under your arms, when your thinnest bit was much further down!

Her hair ribbon was not very neatly tied, but bother that — she was hungry.

Then, when she got downstairs, there was Miss

Gertrude, all alone at the breakfast table, crying! Not her usual snivelling, but floods of tears, and when Louise came in she sprang up, threw her arms round her and exclaimed loudly, 'My poor child!' and 'Oh God, what is to become of us?' and then went on crying louder than ever.

Louise slipped gently out of her embrace as soon as it seemed tactful to do so: she did not like to be touched by people she didn't know very well. She noticed the familiar sinking, rather trembly feeling in her stomach, but she clenched her hands and remained upright – one person moaning was quite enough.

'What is the matter, Miss Gertrude?' she said, calmly.

'Oh, my God, the English... traitors! We shall all be murdered in our beds!'

At that moment Grandfather came in.

'What are you telling the child?' he exclaimed indignantly. 'Pull yourself together, woman! You know Louise is not strong.' He took Louise's hand and she gave his a little squeeze, smiling reassuringly up into his face.

'You tell me what's happened, Grandfather.'

Grandfather's anger vanished as quickly as it had come. 'Just a little misunderstanding, child,' he said kindly. 'The English fleet has been lying off Elsinore for some days, and now Lars has just come down from Smidstrup with the eggs and told us that some Englishmen have landed on the road along the Sound. I don't know what good that will do them,' he added irritably. 'I've never heard of landing soldiers when there has been no declaration of war! There's no need to be frightened, child; no harm has been done, the soldiers just wave to people as they pass. But don't go too far afield today, little one.'

'No, Grandfather,' said Louise obediently. Then she thought of something and asked practically: 'Have you had a proper meal yet this morning, Grandfather?'

Grandfather admitted that he had forgotten all about eating when Lars came, and Louise asked the still sniffing Miss Gertrude to see to it that porridge and eggs were served.

'What a good thing that I've got you!' said Grandfather, when the governess had shut the door behind her. 'That Miss Gertrude is a real moping Minnie!'

Louise chuckled.

'Well, well,' said Grandfather, with a little smile. 'But remember what I said, now – no running around today, stay where you can hear us if we call. The whole thing is probably just a misunderstanding, and the English soldiers are only obeying orders – but at the same time we don't want to invite them in and give them hospitality.'

* * *

Louise had settled herself comfortably in her favourite tree, with the pillow she had brought along behind her head. 'Well brought-up little girls shouldn't climb trees like wild boys!' — but there was no one to scold her today and no one to take her place, either; all of them, apart from the very little ones, had their favourite trees down here on the millstream behind the factory, but Christian was always trying to get to hers first.

It was strange about the soldiers landing; even if it was a misunderstanding, all the same...

Louise admitted frankly to herself that she was frightened. Not the kind of fear you could think through, and understand where it came from, but the worst kind, which buzzed around inside your head so that you simply couldn't think at all.

So it was best to think about something else — something good. Grandfather had told her earlier on that it was a good thing he had her, and he had sounded as if he meant it.

It was a strange feeling, but nice: her being there meant something to somebody; she was no longer just 'one of the children', but a real person.

Grandfather must never find out that I'm frightened, thought Louise. I shall be really sensible and grown-up and make sure that he gets proper meals, and talk to him at table and remind him to have a rest in the afternoon. Whatever happens, no

22

one must ever be able to see that I'm afraid.

It turned out to have been a timely decision.

Louise turned her head – what was that sound? A rhythmic *clonk-clonk*, like a drum beat. And there – she held back a branch just a little, so that she could look out towards the northern road along the beach – there was someone, lots of people, coming! Carrying things that glittered in the sunshine.

The Englishmen were coming, and the glittering things were their guns.

She clasped both hands against her chest to help her hold her breath. Perhaps they would pass by – yes, of course they would pass, they could hardly mean to make war on a solitary grandfather and the few people working in his factory, many of whom were Swedes, at that.

But the soldiers did not pass. She heard the command: 'Halt!' from the road, and someone in a grander uniform dismounted from his horse and walked towards the house with two others.

Louise jumped rather than climbed down from the tree. Then she stopped – first she must decide what to do. Grandfather must be at the factory now, so only Cook and Miss Gertrude were in the house. Miss Gertrude will have a fit! she thought, and giggled a very small giggle, which was no more than a substitute for a scream.

Then she set off at a run for the house – she must

get there first, before Miss Gertrude fetched Grandfather! When they saw that there were no men in the house they would probably move on.

She reached the front door at the same time as the officer and the two soldiers, although she had stopped running when she reached the lilac bushes.

'Good day,' said the officer politely in English, and stopped as she stationed herself in front of the door. 'Oh, I suppose you don't speak English?'

'Yes, I do, but Miss Gertrude doesn't, and we are alone in the house with Cook. You had better go somewhere else.'

The officer smiled. Really, he looked so nice that she could only smile back. 'My name is Wellesley, Arthur Wellesley,' he said, 'and I hadn't thought of staying here long, but I wanted to know if I could leave one or two men here. Is your father far away?' His calm, friendly manner gave Louise a chance to think. 'I'm only a guest here,' she said, forcing herself to smile again.

The officer said that he had thought her English was much too good for her to be Danish, but at the same time Louise heard Grandfather's voice from the other end of the house. 'I can hear the owner of the factory coming,' she said quickly. 'He's nice – but very old!' Then she slipped in through the door before Grandfather caught sight of her.

She stopped just inside, her heart thudding so hard

that the sash tightened round her chest; but surely the officer would not dream of striking an old man? He did not look that sort, but he did believe that she was English, which might turn out to be useful. So she must make sure he did not see her again, because if he were to see her with Grandfather, Grandfather would naturally say that she was his grandchild from St Croix, and certainly Danish!

Louise stayed where she was long enough to hear the officer speaking courteously to Grandfather and Grandfather answering him equally courteously, even if he did not sound particularly friendly – then she slipped silently through the ground floor rooms, out by the garden door and back to her tree by the stream.

Chapter Two

Panting hard, Tim threw himself face down on the bank of the stream. That had been a hot run! Not that the road along the shore was particularly good, either, but having to make his way up hill and down dale through the woods while keeping pace with the soldiers on the road below had certainly not been child's play. True, they had paused once or twice to eat, but the breathing space had been almost worse, because he himself was hungry as a wolf and had eaten all he had with him long before.

Tim sat up and pulled off his shoes and socks; then he put his feet in the water – oh, that felt good!

But what had happened to Uncle Arthur? Tim frowned. It was difficult to decide what was best: that morning he had been too far away, and if a fox had not been snuffling around and woken him up, he would certainly not have heard the boats coming in to land. The sun had been on the point of rising, and it was a splendid sight, with woods and water each as

26

silent as the other – but at the same time strangely eerie; boats filled with soldiers who neither sang nor talked, on their way in to land, where people were sleeping peacefully in their houses, suspecting nothing.

He had followed them when they began to march southwards, staying among the trees so that they could not see him; it was only when they made a halt that he dared go close enough and saw that one of the officers was Uncle Arthur! Most of them must be Germans, because Tim had been unable to understand what they were saying.

He had been on the point of coming out of his hiding-place when he remembered Aunt Isabel; he *had* left a note for her the day before, when he left, saying that he was going into Copenhagen to look at the fleet – but, of course, he had known that she would not like it, otherwise he would certainly not have set off without breakfast!

It was almost unthinkable that the Hero of India could be mean enough to order him home but grown-ups were pretty hard to understand: as soon as there was any excitement you were sent out to play, out of the room, or up to bed – sometimes you would think that grown-ups had children only to have someone to tease. And it was always the same old story: 'It's for your own good, my dear!' 'Your own good' was everything you yourself did not want.

27

So even if he had never envied anyone anything as much as he envied Uncle Arthur his horse, he decided to stay in the wood a while longer and keep pace with them there, on foot. When they had travelled far enough, it probably would not be worth the trouble to send him home.

In any case, Tim was no longer so sure that he did find all this exciting; after all, Admiral Gambier himself had said that they had not declared war on Denmark. There was something underhand about landing soldiers without warning any one.

And he did wish that he knew where that girl had gone — the English girl from yesterday. They had driven off to the south, he had noticed; in a gig, she and some kind of governess, as far as he could see. Now, if she was living with Danish people there was no knowing how they would take it when they discovered what was going on, and if she had been frightened of a mere boy — though she had hidden it as best she could ...

Tim took his feet out of the water, rolled over on his back — and found himself looking straight up into a tree at the very same girl, fast asleep!

He just stopped himself from calling out.

But he had to talk to her. Uncle Arthur had gone into the house down there; perhaps he could take her to Copenhagen with him and get her settled with the English Ambassador, in safety.

28

Tim put his feet back in the water and splashed as loudly as he could; then he began to whistle, quite softly, taking care to keep his eyes on the water all the time.

Up in the tree Louise turned her head sleepily, but it was already getting too hot. She half-opened her eyes, to find the sun shining straight into her face: Lucky she had reinforced the crook where she sat with a mat! But how silly to fall asleep in the middle of the day. There was a bird singing somewhere. No, it could not be a bird, it was a real tune...

Louise leaned forward slightly and found herself looking straight down on the boy's curly red hair. The English boy from yesterday! Tim.

Gently, not letting the branch creak, she leaned back again, so that the leaves of the tree hid her. They had become enemies now!

Ah, but he did not know that, he believed she was English – and the officer believed it too.

Louise thought until her head span. It was the English who were making trade so difficult for Papa, over goods that never arrived – the English who had simply occupied the Virgin Islands, her home, a few years ago, when she was very young. Papa used to sigh and say that of course they had problems themselves, 'with that war-crazy Bonaparte, who wanted to rule the world', but all the same, Denmark was neutral, Denmark had never done anything to

England, other than go to sea and trade. Nevertheless, they had come once before, a long time ago, and stolen ships from Denmark, though the Danes had fought them out on the Sound, and at sea, so bravely that Nelson had had to fool the Crown Prince in order to win. The English actually were our enemies then, thought Louise, and now here they were again, wanting our ships, just like that…and asking Grandfather to invite them to stay here.

There must be something she could do! Should she talk to Tim? Perhaps he knew something, as he had arrived at the same time as the soldiers, something that it might be useful for her to know.

The only thing was that Tim had not done anything; he was decent, and fair, and nice-looking too, with his dark-red, curly hair, and thin, freckled face. There was something dishonest about letting him go on believing that she was not an enemy.

But it couldn't be helped, thought Louise determinedly. It was the English who began this, and if I can get any information so that we can beat them and make them sail home again, I shall do it, even if it is being deceitful!

She peeped out between the leaves, putting a careful little smile on her face. 'Hallo, Tim,' she said.

'Louise!' exclaimed Tim, hoping he sounded surprised. 'What on earth are you doing there?'

'I live here – no, not in this tree, stupid!' Louise replied; then she saw from his face that he was teasing, and laughed herself. 'I'm a guest at the house down there – oh, but, Tim – ' The smile vanished as quickly as it had come – 'Tim, some English soldiers have landed, have you seen them?'

'*Seen* them!' said Tim bitterly. 'I've been running after them, from the moment they came ashore, but through the woods. I feel as if my toes are three times too big for my shoes!'

Louise looked at him in surprise. 'Yes, but why are you hiding from them? They are your countrymen.'

'Thanks very much – they're not only my countrymen: there's my own Uncle Arthur – or half-uncle, in any case, in charge of the company! I can just see him looking down that big nose of his and saying "Tim! You here? Go home to your aunt at once!" When I've been trudging after them since this morning! And I *did* leave a note to say where I was going, but I'm sure he wouldn't even listen: grown-ups never listen!'

'Well, yes,' said Louise practically, 'but you can't know that, until you have spoken to him. Where are you going?'

'I wanted to see the fleet, of course, the two of them. That must be a marvellous sight, because the Danish fleet is famous, you know – and our own is not bad, either,' he added.

'But why are you here, in Denmark? Where does your aunt live?'

'Well, why are *you* here?'

'I was sent here because I had been very ill.' Up to now she had not had to lie; perhaps it wouldn't be necessary to tell a real lie, after all?

'Well, it was the same for me,' said Tim. 'Or rather, not that I was poorly, of course, but my mama had the half-wit...the idea that Bonaparte might arrive in England at any moment and the son and heir had to be taken to safety.' Tim scowled, making Louise want to laugh again, but then his face cleared. 'If Mama only knew that I was right in the middle of it all now! Well, I mean – you know what mothers are like – of all the grown-ups they are the worst fusspots of all. My papa says that he would like to see that ill-bred little Corsican setting foot on English soil, when no one has done that since William the Conqueror!'

That's what happens when you don't think before you speak, thought Tim, annoyed with himself; if only she did not spot the hole in his logic and get frightened! In fact, she was so extraordinarily easy to talk to, you simply did not think of her being a girl, unless you were actually looking at her.

Louise pretended to herself that she had not noticed the shaky feeling in her stomach. 'Only Denmark is not England,' she said quietly, 'and it certainly looks as if England at least can set foot on Danish soil.'

'But we haven't come to make war,' said Tim quickly. 'We're obviously not going to attack a peaceful country — it's just that we *must* have their fleet until we have beaten Bonaparte — and then they'll get it back, you know.'

'Time will show,' said Louise, inwardly amazed at how calmly she could talk about it, once she had pulled herself together. 'It's not so certain that the Danes believe it; and even if they do, I really don't think one can expect them to be particularly happy about it, Tim, not if you're being fair. *We* don't like being ordered about by strangers, do we? And especially — well, when the Danes say that they will definitely not help Napoleon, it's not particularly polite to show that you think they're lying.'

Tim's brow was furrowed. 'But Admiral Gambier said the other day — he's the one who's Commander-in-Chief of our fleet here — he said that a Lord Pembroke had come home and said that the Danes were busy arming their fleet, and it can't be against Napoleon, because he hasn't got a fleet any more — Lord Nelson saw to that!'

'Yes, but that's not true either!' said Louise eagerly, and Tim asked how she could know. Louise answered at once that lots of guests came to the house where she was living at present — 'even if most

33

of them talk about books and poems and the theatre – and about the freedom of the press as well.'

'So you understand some Danish?' asked Tim.

Louise wished she could sink into the ground. Tim's brown eyes were looking at her so honestly and trustfully, as if he could never believe anyone was lying.

The fleet! she thought. Remember the fleet! 'Oh yes, I know some,' she said.

'Are they angry with you now?' Tim asked cautiously. 'I mean –'

Louise stopped him before he could say 'because you are English', which would mean that she could not protest. 'No, certainly not,' she said energetically. 'My ... my host, Mr Drewsen, is terribly, terribly nice and kind to everyone. After all, he knows perfectly well that there is nothing I can do about it. Tim, that must have been your uncle I was talking to earlier; nothing will happen to old Mr Drewsen, will it?'

She was frightened, after all, though she sounded so sensible, so it was lucky he could answer that one right away.

'No, of course not!' he said angrily. 'No decent person could possibly go and upset an old gentleman! Do you realize that Uncle Arthur is actually the Hero of India?'

Louise thought to herself that this did not make

things any better: did they really need to send *heroes* over here to give orders? But she could scarcely say that aloud.

'But he said he wanted to have some men staying here – living here – he is not staying himself. And if they are sailors...' She had said yesterday that she was afraid of sailors, though there was no knowing why she was more afraid of them than of other people, but he could see that her eyes had turned a very dark blue.

'Of course they won't be sailors! Really, *girls*!' said Tim, sounding thoroughly resigned. 'Sailors don't run around on land, you little silly! It will just be a look-out post or something like that – and Uncle Arthur is awfully bright. What I said about him sending me home to Aunt Isabel is just one of those things grown-ups always do. In fact, he's actually – yes, he is! And if this Mr Drewsen is a nice old gentleman, you can rely on Uncle Arthur to see that and to make sure that they're decent people.'

Tim hesitated a moment. 'If you like, I can come out of hiding and talk to Uncle Arthur about it myself,' he said, trying not to sound as self-sacrificing as he felt.

Louise said that would not be necessary. 'It's enough for you to have told me – otherwise you're running the risk of your uncle sending you home to your aunt. Listen, are you hungry?'

Tim had been chewing on one blade of grass after another.

'I'm practically dying of hunger,' he said frankly. 'And thirst!'

'Climb up my tree, and I'll go and get you something.'

And before he could look round, she had gone.

Louise looked warily through the window into the garden-room; it was empty. She slipped quickly into the passage to the kitchen, where Sophie was drinking coffee with Lars, the coachman. They were chattering away so hard that the coffee was almost splashing into their saucers. Even with a lump of sugar between their teeth, they carried on with their 'And then he saw...' 'Yes, and she saw the gentleman waving his hands about...' '...ah, but you can't understand a word they say...' 'But if I've got to look after those monkeys, I shall need at least two girls down from Springforbye ... or my sisters from Taarbaek...'

Then Sophie caught sight of Louise waiting impatiently for a pause in the chatter. 'Miss Louise! My dear child... oh Lord, what's happened *now*?'

Louise said it was just that she was hungry, and could she please have some food and some fruit juice to take outside, 'because the weather is so lovely and Grandfather is busy, so he won't be eating till later.'

'Well, for heaven's sake!' Sophie put aside the brimming saucer and went to the larder for bread and slices of ham. 'There's a bit of fried chicken here, too, if you like, Miss Louise?'

Louise said 'yes, thank you,' and Sophie got a basket and filled it with good food, the skilful hands working away regardless of Lars Coachman, who had begun to chatter all over again. The final addition was a bowl of raspberries and thick cream, arranged so that they could not spill.

'Lars can carry it out for you, Miss Louise,' she said.

Louise refused hastily. 'Lars is probably busy too, and it's so beautifully packed, I can manage on my own,' and she had grasped the basket before they could protest.

And after all that, there was Tim, sitting up in her tree, fast asleep! Well, he had been up very early. Louise spread out the white napkin on a flat patch of grass and unpacked and laid out the feast before calling him. 'You can come down now. Practically nobody ever comes here except us children.'

'Mmm'mm!' went Tim from above, and dropped down in a flash.

Half-way through the meal he looked up. 'Aren't you hungry? Wouldn't you like some of this chicken?'

Louise took a little, because watching Tim made

her hungry; one would think he had had nothing to eat for days!

'Why do you think there would be a look-out post here?' she asked thoughtfully. 'There are no ships, only the fishing boats from Taarbaek sail past here.'

Tim explained with his mouth full that the English had brought lots of soldiers with them. 'They are to stay in different places outside Copenhagen, you see, so the town will be cut off and no one will be able to get food in. That way the Danes will be forced to give up – when there is no food left, I mean!'

'That sounds... wicked!' said Louise slowly. 'It doesn't sound fair!'

Tim sighed and gulped down more lemonade. 'I suppose it's difficult to be at war and be fair at the same time,' he said, 'but it's better to make them give up that way than having to bomb the town...'

'Bomb it!' Louise exclaimed, horrified. 'But, Tim, it's a *town*! You ... I ... you mean with *bombs*? Setting houses on fire? But, Tim, *people* live in those houses, real people, I mean, not soldiers... You surely can't believe that anyone would want to drop bombs on a real town, so that the houses burn and people are burned to death – children and everything, people who have done nothing wrong...'

Tim nodded, too wretched to speak.

Louise jumped up, as white as a sheet. 'I don't believe it! No one could do anything so wicked!

38

How could you bear to be English and live, knowing that your own people, your own fathers or brothers, could think of doing anything so wicked!'

Chapter Three

'No one says it's always easy, either, my dear.' The voice came from the bush in whose shade they were sitting, and then someone appeared from behind it.

'Uncle Arthur!' gasped Tim.

The officer stood looking at them for a moment, but it was impossible to see from his face what he was thinking. 'Shall we sit down again?' he suggested, because Tim had also jumped up, almost overturning the bowl of raspberries.

Louise and Tim sat down again on the grass, close together, and Uncle Arthur sat facing them.

'If there are any raspberries left when you have finished, I would love to try them,' he said. 'But I suppose there won't be...'

The two of them looked suspiciously at him; the gap between bombs and raspberries was too great for them to leap all at once. But perhaps he was really hungry, thought Louise, and Papa said that an uninvited guest was still a guest, as long as he was in one's house and behaved politely.

'There is a little lemonade left anyway, sir,' she said. 'Can you drink from the pitcher, because Tim has used the glass?'

Uncle Arthur said that if Tim was fit enough to go adventuring without permission he was certainly not suffering from anything catching.

'Sir!' Tim began indignantly, but Uncle Arthur broke in: 'I know, Tim, I have heard all about it. You left a note for your aunt saying where you had gone, so we must hope it will soothe her,' he added ironically.

'Sir!' Tim began again.

'Be quiet, Tim. I cannot worry about Isabel's auntly problems now, I have more important things to do. In any case, I have never believed in your mother's idea of you as a delicate plant that should be kept wrapped in cotton wool. Any normal boy would have done exactly the same thing, and I have no intention of putting a spoke in your wheel – *provided* that you are sensible and think what you are doing, *and* give me your word that you will clear out immediately, if – if what you were talking about here should really come to pass.'

He turned his head and looked at Louise, and quite suddenly she liked him. He was a little awe-inspiring to look at, with that weather-beaten face and great hook-nose, but his eyes were grave, and he spoke as if he took it for granted that even if you were only a child, you could still use your brains.

'Look here, Louise, you and Tim are not the only ones who are horrified by the thought of bombing a peaceful town full of peaceful people. Most people at home in England would feel the same, and even we, who have been sent here, don't like it, but we do know something about this Bonaparte which perhaps you do not know. Shall I try to explain?'

Louise nodded without speaking.

'It began with a revolution. Dangerous things, revolutions. They may sound just, to start with, but before you can get your bearings they have ended in turmoil, with everyone distrusting everyone else. Then people begin to strike out right and left, and there is always one who can hit harder than the rest. Suddenly he is in complete control, with all the power that the revolution was meant to distribute more fairly – and he's always greedy to use it.

'Bonaparte is such a man. If he had started creating order in France, so that people had a better life, there would have been no war. But instead he began to conquer other countries, one by one, and give them to members of his own family to rule. Soon there will be only Scandinavia left and, of course, England. But we don't want him in England, do we, Louise? England is ours, it must not fall into

Bonaparte's hands. That's why we have to go to war, we must stop him swallowing up the world.'

'And that's why we *must* take over the Danish fleet, so that it cannot be used against us. Can you understand that?'

Louise considered for a long time. It was so unusual to have a grown-up – and a hero to boot! – talking to one about anything but dolls and lessons.

'I can understand most of it,' she said at last, 'except for the last part, because Denmark would never let Nap ... Bonaparte, I mean, have the fleet. Everyone who comes to this house says so, and Tim says Bonaparte has no fleet, so he couldn't just take it, could he?'

'But he could come up from the south with his soldiers and take the country,' said Uncle Arthur, 'and then the Danish fleet would be his as well.'

Louise bit her lip: she could see very well that there was no answer to that.

'But the *rockets*, Uncle Arthur!' cried Tim. 'Soldiers have to fight, of course, if there is something it's necessary to fight for. The rockets are what we think so ghastly.'

Uncle Arthur said irritably that no one liked it, he had said so already.

'Why do you think I am sitting here drinking lemonade? We are putting things off as long as we possibly can, but by now they must be unloading the horses up at Vibek, or whatever it's called. I'm going to wait for General Cathcart and the Dragoons, and then we must push on towards the town. In any case, I don't know why on earth the Danes don't get a move on! Up to now we've been sauntering along as if we were going for a walk in the woods!'

'Yes, but *I* know!' said Louise eagerly. 'It's because there has been no declaration of war, my... my host, old Mr Drewsen, says, and my other host, too, who is his son. And General Peymann certainly does not want to be the one to attack the English, so there you are!'

'But what about the Crown Prince?' exclaimed Uncle Arthur in surprise. 'The king is still sick, isn't he? Where the devil is the Crown Prince − sorry, I mean, where is the Crown Prince? Has Jackson met him, or not?'

Louise was about to reply, but then she stopped herself. Everything that Tim's uncle had said sounded reasonable, and he did not know that he was questioning a Danish girl, he thought she was English. But she *was* Danish. The fleet had to be used to keep an eye on all the cargo ships, it was simply impossible to let the English have it. How was she to get out of this?

Then, suddenly, she knew.

'I don't think there's anything I can say,' she said, not realizing that she was squeezing her hands together in her lap. 'The Drewsens are so nice, and so kind to me and Mr Drewsen's son has gone to Copenhagen to help defend the fleet – I simply *can't* gossip about it and perhaps even help to get him killed, when I'm living in his house!'

Tim's uncle looked at her, frowning, and did not answer.

'Please understand, sir,' she said, dismayed to hear her voice shaking.

Uncle Arthur's frown disappeared. 'Yes,' he said slowly. 'I must say I wish you were my daughter. For goodness sake don't tell me who your father is – I'm beginning to get an idea and it would be best for me not to know who you are. Tell me, do you know Tim well enough to rely on what he tells you?'

Tim held his breath, expecting her to say that she had known him for one hour in all. That was the truth, after all, so it would be foolish to mind hearing her say it.

Louise looked from Tim's uncle to Tim and back again. 'Yes, I know him well enough,' she said.

Uncle Arthur was looking terribly serious now, but his voice was quite calm. 'Tim, tell Louise what you know about me. Not that rubbish about the Hero of India and all that, but if you believe that I will do all I can to ensure that not a single Dane is harmed, tell Louise so.'

Tim pondered for a few moments, while Louise

sat waiting, her eyes on his face.

'Once,' he said, 'once I had a scratch that got inflamed and swelled up. Of course the doctor and Mama and all the rest of them said it wouldn't hurt a bit to have it lanced, but I didn't believe them. Then Uncle Arthur chased them all out, except for the doctor, and said he didn't suppose I was stupid enough not to realize that it would hurt quite a bit. Then he held my hand while it was done – I was very young then, of course – and said I could howl if I liked, he wouldn't tell anyone.'

'And you didn't howl,' said Tim's uncle with a grin. 'Your eyes were full of tears, but that is what happens if something hurts badly enough, and it's not at all the same as howling. But I don't know if that story means anything to Louise?'

But Louise had already made her decision.

'I don't know very much, so it may mean nothing,' she said seriously. 'Sometimes you get tired of grown-ups talking and you stop listening. An Englishman did go to the Crown Prince and threaten him, down in Kiel. They said he was terribly rude, so the Crown Prince was angry. He – the Crown Prince, that is – *was* in Copenhagen, but only for two days. General Peymann is the one who is going to defend the town, and the fleet too, I imagine – or perhaps that was someone else?'

'Have you ever seen the general?'

46

'No, but old Mr Drewsen has, or perhaps it was just someone who knew him.'

Tim's uncle frowned again and said, as if to himself, 'But if he is in command, why the devil has he done nothing? The man cannot believe that we shall not advance if he does not lift a finger to stop us!'

'Yes, but General Peymann says he has always understood that an army does not land between two fortresses, Mr Drewsen's son says.'

'Good Lord above, what an almighty idiot he must be!' exclaimed Uncle Arthur.

Louise retorted angrily that he was not an idiot at all. Tim's uncle gave her a searching look and she felt her cheeks turn red; of course she must not keep on defending all the Danes. 'Well, I don't really know, of course: they say he's a nice old gentleman, but he's even older than old Mr Drewsen, it's really hard on him that the Crown Prince just looked in for two days and ordered him to defend Copenhagen at all costs, and then left again, leaving everything to an old man – but the Crown Prince does think he himself always knows best...'

One could criticize the Crown Prince all right, the adults sometimes did that themselves, when they were talking about the freedom of the press, and all that.

'Good Lord above!' cried Uncle Arthur again.

'Louise, what else do they say about the Crown Prince in this house?'

Louise thought about it. 'Well, everyone says that he means well and is hard-working and that kind of thing, and conscientious. And they say he doesn't always know what's important and what isn't and that it's a shame old Count Bernstorff is dead, because when *he* said something the Crown Prince listened.'

'H'm. Louise, who else comes to the house? The owner of the factory seems to be a fine old gentleman.'

Louise said that there were Mr and Mrs Rahbek, and Mrs Rahbek's sister, Miss Heger, and their brothers and sisters.

Uncle Arthur said names were no good. 'They mean nothing to me. Do you know what influence these people have? Do you think any of them could reach General Peymann with a message?'

'Well, Mr Rahbek was a professor until recently, but he's captain of the Students' Corps, I think.' Louise had a bright idea: 'But then there is my... my host, Mr Drewsen – not old Mr Drewsen, of course, but his son. He's a lieutenant, or perhaps it's called first lieutenant, in something they call the militia.'

'Good. Could you keep quiet for a bit and let me think.'

Tim was about to say that they weren't making a

sound, but then he looked at Uncle Arthur's face and changed his mind.

What an extraordinary girl Louise was! So much for those cousins of his at home, who always said girls were stupid and good for nothing but talk of gowns and giggling! Uncle Arthur had obviously seen at once that Louise was not like that at all. Tim had been feeling rather left out, because Uncle Arthur had been talking to Louise all the time, but of course she was the one who had been in Denmark longest and knew things – he himself had only arrived a few weeks ago.

By way of apology he picked up the raspberry bowl, looked at Louise, who nodded, and pushed it into Uncle Arthur's hand. The soldier took it without turning his head, and began to eat.

When he had finished all the raspberries he looked at the young people and smiled, but both Louise and Tim could see that his eyes were not smiling.

'Now, this is my idea,' he said. 'It must be a complete secret between the three of us and General Cathcart, because I dare not think of all the trouble I shall get into, and with good reason, if we are found out. But from everything Louise has told me I can see that Copenhagen is in very serious danger – very! We have brought over Congreve's Rockets – Tim can tell you about them; they are disgustingly effective horrors. If I can get a message through to General

Peymann, we may be able to save the town; I can't imagine that he would pay any attention to the Crown Prince's frivolous orders when he hears what the rockets can do.'

Tim jumped up. 'Let me go, sir!' he said eagerly. 'No one would notice a boy.'

'Do you speak Danish, Tim?'

'No, not many words. "Thank you very much," and that kind of thing,' Tim confessed, crestfallen.

'And you, Louise?'

'Quite a lot,' said Louise, surprised that her voice did not seem to be trembling.

'Tim's right that no soldiers, either English or Danish, would notice a boy, and the same applies to *two* boys. Tim would take good care of you and make sure nothing happens to you. Would you dare to go to Copenhagen with him and find young Mr Drewsen?'

Louise had completely forgotten about the fleet; she was thinking about the bombs, houses burning, other children screaming and terrified. Then she looked into Tim's eyes.

'Yes,' she said.

Chapter Four

Tim shifted for the umpteenth time on his perch in Louise's tree. Surely it would be dark soon!

He had slept for at least four hours that afternoon, and longer in the woods, because Uncle Arthur had said that Louise must stay indoors for quite a long time so that her governess and the old gentleman would know where she was; and also that it would be a good idea for Tim to get some sleep, since he had been up so early, and they would have to wait for Louise's bedtime before leaving. 'I would never get permission from Mr Drewsen,' she had said, 'I shall have to go without asking.'

Uncle Arthur had planned the whole thing; first he had asked if the old gentleman could *read* as well as speak English and Louise had said she thought he could, because he used to do business with two Englishmen, who had once lived nearby and who were also paper manufacturers. 'Then I shall write a few lines to your host, so that he knows you have not left out of sheer mischief. He will be angry, and I can well understand that, but I am the one he will be angry with.'

Louise had taken the letter with her, to leave on her pillow just before she went out. Tim also had a letter in his pocket, for young Mr Drewsen.

Timothy Brandon is a young relative of mine. I would ask you to listen very closely to what the two children have to tell you.
Arthur Wellesley, Major General.

Tim ran through the plan in his head. Louise was to find some boy's clothes to wear; she said that would be quite easy, because Mr Drewsen had a son of twelve. Then she was to see if she could smuggle out some food and a bottle of water. Water was important, Uncle Arthur said; it was better to be hungry than thirsty. If she had a little money that she could take with her, it would help.

'You must keep yourselves to yourselves as much as possible, but you will probably have to buy a little food on the way. The journey is sure to take some days as you must avoid places where there are soldiers. Louise only knows the direct road into town. Buy your food from farmers' wives in *small* farmhouses – it will probably be less obvious to them that you are not Danish.'

After Louise had gone in Tim had received a stream of instructions and warnings, until he became impatient and said he knew very well that he was to take great care of Louise.

Uncle Arthur had apologised at once. 'It's not because I'm in any doubt about that,' he said, 'but you are old enough to know that what I'm doing is very wrong. Just think what your mother would say, or Aunt Isabel: I'm *enticing* a young girl, who is clearly used to being looked after and protected, to run away from home with a perfectly strange boy, to disguise herself in boy's clothes, to enter a besieged town. The thought of what your mother would say makes me shudder!'

Tim could not help grinning at the idea of Uncle Arthur being afraid of Mama – Uncle Arthur, the hero of Argaum and Gawilghur! But of course it was quite true that there would be a fearful uproar if anyone ever found out – and Mama would certainly think the boy's clothes were the worst of it, thought Tim.

'But I cannot imagine anything happening to you, as long as you behave sensibly. The Danes here, outside Copenhagen, are not at all sure what is going on and we ourselves will negotiate until we are blue in the face before opening the attack. The soldiers have very strict orders, stating that they are on a peaceful mission, and if with your help and Louise's we can come out of this in peace, then I cannot be too bothered about a little girl's being obliged to do something "unsuitable". This Louise is an extraordinary girl, because she knew perfectly well what she was agreeing to do! But, Tim, that doesn't mean she won't be frightened; can you try to remember that people who do something that scares them are actually braver than those who are *not* frightened. Oh Lord, if only I knew whether what I am doing is right!'

Tim was sure it was; they would manage. Then he and Uncle Arthur looked for a good place where two horses could be left for them; Uncle Arthur would speak to Lord Cathcart and tell him about the plan so that the horses would be ready. He wondered if Louise had ever ridden without a side-saddle before?

'I think you're tired, Grandfather,' said Louise, taking away the book that had lain idle in her grandfather's hand.

He sighed and said it was true: it had been a long day.

'Draw the curtains, child.' This was not their custom, but Louise understood quite well what he meant. Things were different now, there were strangers outside – well, not right outside, but all the same, things felt different.

'Is there anything you need, Grandfather? A cup of tea, perhaps?'

Her grandfather looked up, slightly astonished, and then smiled kindly. 'Oh, I don't know. I expect Cook has gone to bed, and Miss Gertrude, too. It must be your bedtime, isn't it? You've been sitting so quietly with your sewing, keeping me company.'

Louise smiled again, with a bad conscience. 'But I can easily make you some tea, Grandfather,' she said. 'If I put a drop of rum in it, you're sure to sleep well.'

Grandfather's worried frown seemed to relax a little. 'Thank you, my dear – if you think you can manage.'

The big kitchen was dark and silent. Louise quickly lit a small lamp and used the bellows to rekindle the fire in the stove enough to boil a little water. Cup and saucer on a tray, two good slices of the best, yellowest cake – and all the time she was hating what she did. Her grandfather was old. She had never thought of it before, but as he sat in there his age showed – and he was lonely too. For the first time in her life she, Louise, could have been somebody, could have looked after her grandfather, done little things for him, and kept him company.

Instead of that, she was deceiving and deserting him. A tear fell on a slice of cake, but it would not leave any taste – and there was no time for regrets.

Better to remember that it was precisely in order to help that she had to deceive him.

Louise wiped the next tear away impatiently. While the water was coming to the boil she would collect some food in a basket, ready to take with them. A long sausage, a whole loaf, fresh cheese – did she dare to take a jar of preserved strawberries? Tim would love them, but glass would not be a good thing to take riding. Ah, there was a whole dish of pigeon pies that Cook had made yesterday! Louise took four – and then there was the bottle of water – she had nearly forgotten that.

Now for a clean cloth to cover the food. And a knife! By now the water was boiling, and Louise made the tea, arranged the tray and carried it in carefully – it would be just her luck if she dropped it and awakened Miss Gertrude! She would have to leave the doors open behind her, otherwise the cup would tip.

'Ah! That was a good idea, my dear,' said Grandfather contentedly, when he had added a little rum to the tea and swallowed the first mouthful. 'You're not frightened, are you, my child? There is nothing to be afraid of. I had some talk with this Major General Wellesley – a pleasant man, whom I would have been glad to see in my house in different circumstances. He explained England's difficulties to me – and the Englishman who went to see the

56

Crown Prince obviously misunderstood his mission. They will sort it out now, you'll see.'

All this sounded a little as if Grandfather were talking to reassure himself as well. Louise thought of the rockets – Uncle Arthur would not have said anything about them. It was better not to mention them now, because Grandfather had enough to think about already. Aloud, she said that it really must be her bedtime.

'You should go to bed, too, Grandfather.'

Her grandfather nodded and put his hand out to her. Wondering a little, Louise rose and put her hand in his. He held it firmly and lifted his face to hers.

He wanted her to kiss him on the cheek!

Respectfully, Louise pressed her lips against the wrinkled cheek in a place where there was no beard. Then she whispered, 'Good night, Grandfather,' and ran out of the room before her eyes filled with tears again.

As she had thought, Carl's clothes were the ones that fitted best. They were still a little too large, but that was better than being too small. The trousers were too wide in the waist, but she had a scarf she could tie round them. What else did boys wear? A shirt, yes, and then that short jacket. Louise could not remember if the collar of the shirt should be inside or outside, but Tim would know. And a hat!

In her own room she tried on the hat in front of the

mirror; it was not easy to stuff all her hair into the crown – she had better take a pair of scissors so that Tim could cut some of it off, if it turned out to hang down too far – and Carl's shoes were quite impossibly large, she would have to keep her own shoes, but without ribbons.

When she had folded the blue scarf and tied it round her waist outside the shirt and trousers, she felt she could very well pass for a boy.

Tim was not so sure, when he first saw her in the moonlight; it did not seem natural for a boy to be so pretty, or at least he knew none who were, but it would be best not to tell her that.

'Everything all right?' he asked in a whisper, taking the basket from her.

Louise nodded. At the pond she turned and looked back. Everything was in darkness, the workers' homes, the factory, the house up there, and so silent without the rush of water round the mill wheel.

Tim took her hand. 'Come on!'

Uncle Arthur had thought of everything. The horses were the smallest that could be found, but they were still pretty big, so they had been tied up close to a good, solid tree-stump, with the help of which it was not too difficult to get into the saddle. Louise said nothing about being unused to riding without a side-saddle, and she had actually thought of a sugar-lump each for the horses!

'We can take the road for the first stretch,' said Tim. 'After that we shall have to ride through the woods, because Uncle Arthur said that General Baird would be marching along the coast road with his people to somewhere called Charlottenlund – but we mustn't go too far inland, either, because the central column is not far away – General Ludlow reckoned on reaching Jaegersborg this evening, and that's quite close to here, isn't it?'

Louise thought for a moment and then said she thought it would be better for them to turn into the woods at once. 'In case there is anyone at the quarantine station.'

On the first stretch they did not speak. The horses seemed quiet enough, and Tim rode ahead, setting such an easy pace that the horses had time to see where they were stepping.

'What are their names?' asked Louise in a low voice, when they had been riding for some time.

Uncle Arthur had forgotten to tell them that, or perhaps he had not known. 'Well, they have to have names,' said Louise, 'otherwise we shan't be able to call them.'

This led to a good deal of joking; Tim suggested all kinds of silly names and Louise kept pace with him – which was just as Tim had intended…she had looked so serious almost as long as he had known her.

'We'll call them Lise and Lasse,' said Louise at last. 'They had better have Danish names, in case someone hears us talking to them.'

Then Tim told her about his own horse at home and about the place where he lived. Louise asked what it looked like, and he tried to describe the landscape and Brandon Hall, a white house shining in the midst of green lawns that ran down to the river.

In a little while he'll be asking me where *I* live, thought Louise in a panic. I must say something quickly, talk about something else.

'Do you like living in the country best?' she asked. 'It's exciting in town for the first few days, but you get tired of it quite quickly, or I do. All the things you're not allowed to do in town! And it's so boring, paying calls!'

'Yes, well, boys don't have to do that,' said Tim. 'On the other hand, the grown-ups, the men I mean, do so many exciting things that I'm not old enough to do.'

I suppose she doesn't want to tell me where she lives, Tim was thinking. Now, why not? But if so, it would be polite to talk about something else. 'You will tell me when you get tired, won't you? Then we'll find a good place.'

Louise said she thought they could keep going as far as 'Sea Joy'. 'There's a mound down near the beach, with some good big trees on it, and a poet who comes to the Drewsens says Count Schimmelmann's family is very nice. So they won't be cross, even if they find us.'

She probably liked the idea of being near a house, thought Tim. So she *was* afraid of the dark, after all, even if she did not show it.

But it would not do: he was sure Uncle Arthur would say it was a bad idea.

'I think we should sleep as far as possible from places where people live,' he objected cautiously. 'The horses must be given a long tether so that they can graze, and if any of the servants are about early, before we wake up...'

Louise said obligingly that in that case he had better choose the spot. 'But we mustn't ride further than that, or we shall be too close to Charlottenlund, I think.'

In fact she was also getting very sore, sitting astride this big horse for so long, but she had no intention of saying anything about that!

Fortunately it was not long before Tim stopped. 'These bushes will give us good cover, the trees will shelter us from the sun when it gets up in the morning and there's a tree-stump over there for when we have to mount again tomorrow. Do you think you would be afraid to sleep here?'

'What is there to be afraid of?' Louise sounded surprised.

61

'Oh well, the dark...' said Tim hesitantly. Would anyone ever understand girls? But of course, Louise was no ordinary sort of girl.

'The dark can't hurt us,' she said practically. 'It's only a coverlet that the earth pulls over itself when it sleeps. At least that's what Dolly always said – she's our nursemaid. Underneath, everything is just the same as it is by day.'

Chapter Five

Tim took care of the horses while Louise unrolled the two rugs that had been strapped to the saddles. The food basket she set between them, but they agreed it would be best to go to sleep at once and keep the food for the morning. So they drank a little water and helped each other to roll up in their rugs.

Tim lay awake for quite a time after they had said good night. Up to now everything had gone smoothly enough, but all the same it was a bit of a – yes, responsibility! They were completely on their own. Uncle Arthur, who had been leading the right wing of the brigade, must be far inland by now; there was no one to tell them what was happening in Copenhagen and neither of them knew how best to approach the town itself. Louise knew only the East Gate, and that must be close to the Sound, so that road, at all events, was impossible. And at some point they might also bump into some Danish defensive positions. Unless the old general was completely stupid, he must at least have manned the ramparts.

If he had been alone – but he had Louise to take care of, and he had given Uncle Arthur his word that he would hand her over to this Mr Drewsen or some other grown-up whom she knew.

'The English Ambassador will not do,' Uncle Arthur had said. 'Garlike has been ordered to Berlin, and the new one, Brook Taylor, is quite a different type. I would not trust him to take charge of a little girl in this situation.'

At the same time, Tim had had to promise to leave Copenhagen quickly, the very moment the bombing began – if, that is, the negotiations came to nothing. Grown-ups! thought Tim resignedly; they were totally unreasonable, the lot of them, even Uncle Arthur. One thing was certain: if he was forced to choose, he would pay no attention to the bombardment. She had said yes, she could rely on his word, and yes, she did dare to go into Copenhagen alone with him, although she knew there were soldiers everywhere; he would rather let himself be blown up than lose sight of her before he had handed her over to Mr Drewsen, and Uncle Arthur could say what he liked, afterwards!

She turned over again; he was sure she was not asleep either.

'Why are you so frightened of sailors?' he asked quietly. 'That is, if you can talk about it.'

Perhaps she would be able to talk about it, here in

the darkness, and when it was to Tim.

'I – I don't even think I know, exactly,' she said hesitantly, speaking as softly as he had. 'It probably just sounds silly. You see, Mr Drewsen – not old Mr Drewsen, I mean, but his son – knew a captain called Jensen, a Dane. He had just taken his ship to the West Indian islands owned by Denmark, to keep an eye on the merchant ships, now there is so much war everywhere. He is very brave and has fought a good many privateers and even some real English warships…actually he is a nice man and of course it was only because the boys thought it was so exciting that he told stories about all the fights with other ships. But it sounded so…so terrible, and then when I was so ill with inflammation of the lungs that they all thought I was going to die, I started dreaming about all the ships burning and people being shot by cannons, or drowning because they couldn't swim. Often they had their arms blown off, or legs…Well, I didn't die, but I've got into a habit of going weak inside when something unexpected happens. And sometimes I dream about it all over again. Of course, I know it's terribly feeble,' she finished despondently, 'but I can't help it.'

Tim said he could not see anything feeble about it. 'It's not the kind of thing you tell girls about,' he added angrily.

Louise was silent for a while; then she said

cautiously: 'But do you think it's the kind of thing you talk to boys about, Tim? I mean – of course people have to defend themselves if they are attacked, but it seems to me that in a war both sides are doing terrible things, not something they should be expecting children to find exciting.'

'No, of course it's not,' said Tim slowly, 'not when you really think about it. I think you should try to remember it as little as possible. Go to sleep now and think instead about trying to reach Mr Drewsen, so that he can stop that kind of thing happening here in Denmark.'

Louise nodded in the darkness. 'It actually feels as if it's helped to tell you about it. Sleep well, Tim.'

Tim lay awake a little longer, remembering that he had never been able to make Uncle Arthur talk about war, but Cousin James was a different matter – and what about Uncle Robert? They had known all about the various battles and had volunteered to go as soon as they could lie convincingly about their age. Yes, but Uncle Robert, when he had come home a little while ago because he had been wounded – he hadn't talked about war any more then. In fact he seemed to want to forget about it and talk about something else. Perhaps both he and Uncle Arthur knew that Louise was right.

*   *   *

The next morning Louise was woken up by someone tickling her cheek with a blade of grass. She opened her eyes and looked straight up into Tim's freckled, smiling face. 'I'm frightfully hungry,' he said cheerfully. 'Couldn't you wake up now?'

Louise sat up. The sun was shining down between the trees, the horses were grazing peacefully a little way off – and it was quite true, sleeping out in the woods made you terribly hungry.

'We must stop now, Tim,' she said, licking her fingers clean. 'Otherwise there'll be nothing left!'

Tim said that the food would not keep long in this heat anyway, and it would be a shame if they had to throw anything away. 'Those pigeon pies taste marvellous, don't they? And I have got some money, only I don't know quite what things cost. I've only got six marks...'

'Are you mad!' exclaimed Louise. 'That's a whole *Speciedaler*, it's lots of money, ninety-six shillings! So we'll certainly be able to manage. I only had one *Rigsdaler* left, because I gave Emily money to buy me new ribbons in Copenhagen, because I was out of light blue and yellow ones. But we'll manage all right!'

That was all very well, Tim thought, but there was no knowing how long it would take them to reach the capital – especially when they were meant to talk to people as little as possible.

He asked if she really didn't know the names of any places outside Copenhagen.

'There's Hellerupgaard,' said Louise, 'where Erichsen, the government agent, lives. And then there's Dronninggaard, but we are closer to Copenhagen than that; oh yes, and then of course there's Hill House, where Mr and Mrs Rahbek live. Mr Drewsen is Mrs Rahbek's uncle. But the places I know are mostly ones where people live in the summer,' Louise ended, a little downcast.

Tim said that was quite all right. What else could he say?

They really did seem to be getting on better than he had expected on that first night, thought Tim a day or two later, when they stopped to eat their supper. Louise had certainly not been exaggerating when she said she could speak some Danish! As far as he could hear, she sounded exactly like the Danes who came to visit his aunt Isabel – and she was fantastically good at making up stories!

On the very first day she had invented a story about two brothers on their way to the capital to tell their father that English soldiers had arrived at their home and their mother did not know what to do, because she was ill and had to keep to her bed.

Louise told this story quite coolly every time they

were asked how a couple of boys could have been allowed to wander around on their own in these uncertain times. She had cut her scarf in two and tied one half round Tim's neck, so that if anyone spoke to him first because he looked older, she could say that he had caught a sore throat from their mother and could not say a word.

Tim was rather uncomfortable with a cloth round his neck in the heat, but Louise just said: 'Well, it's no worse than this jacket I've got to ride around in.'

And it was quite clear that the story worked well; everyone felt sorry for them, and the day before yesterday, when it had begun to rain, a nice woman had even asked them indoors and given them a little room for the night.

Tim thought dismally that the only job he had to do was to look after the horses and, of course, be there to keep an eye on Louise.

Well, that was what Uncle Arthur had ordered him to do, and for Heaven's sake, it was quite childish to be annoyed because he could not play the hero! The important thing was for them to get to Copenhagen with Uncle Arthur's message.

Anxiety went on gnawing at Tim's mind. The time! They were certainly managing very well on their own account; there were no problems with the horses, nor with finding food – in fact they were not even always allowed to pay for it – and Louise was as tough as any boy, thought Tim, though she looked so small and frail that one would not have believed those little white hands could hold anything more wayward than a bunch of wild flowers. Not one moan had there been – in fact, she was much better than a boy, because she did not get mulish when he knew more about something than she did; she would just say: 'Oh well, if you *know* that, we'll do as you say.'

But they really should have reached the town by now. Tim was sure they were riding on a zigzag course and wasting far too much time because they did not know where they were. One little village was much like another, he thought, and what good did it do to know the name of the one they were riding through, when they did not even know if they were riding in the right direction? When Louise asked, people would just give the name of another village and point along the road: but what if they came to a place where the road forked later on? There was one thing they did know: the sun rose in the east and set in the west; but for the rest of the day it was simply up there in the sky – and yesterday the sky had been overcast as well.

Suddenly, as if she could guess what he was thinking, Louise said: 'What are we to do, Tim? Time is passing – how long do you think Uncle

Arthur and the others can go on spinning it out? Perhaps we are too late already! Why on earth don't I know more about the towns and villages...'

She looked so upset that Tim told her there was no way she could have known she would need to know them.

'Perhaps we should simply have followed the soldiers, instead of turning away as soon as we heard there were some in the neighbourhood,' she said doubtfully. 'At least we would have been sure of taking the right road.'

Tim swallowed some water and replaced the cork firmly. 'Oh yes! And absolutely sure that as soon as they caught sight of us we would not get a step further! The foot-soldiers might not have taken any notice, but there is always an officer around and he would be quite certain to say it was his duty to make sure that we did not go into any village he might be bombarding later on!'

'In that case we might have shown him the letter from Uncle Arthur,' Louise suggested.

'A letter from an English major general to a Danish lieutenant!' exclaimed Tim. 'Louise, think! Would you have Uncle Arthur condemned for treason?'

She gave him a startled look. 'But your uncle did say that — that England and Denmark were not at war.'

71

'Oh yes, that was then! The way we are zigzagging about now — we don't know a thing about it! We're keeping well away from English troops, I'll have you know. And if disaster strikes, you just speak *Danish*, and I have a sore throat!'

'I won't be ordered about!' said Louise hotly. 'I never said anything when I could see you were right, but don't talk to me like that. Otherwise you can look out for yourself, so there!'

'Sorry,' said Tim sulkily. Then his sense of justice took over.   'I – I didn't mean to order you about, it's just that...'

'... that both of us are worried,' Louise interrupted, smiling at him. 'I'm so frightened that – well, you know – that we're not going to get there, before...'

They sat in silence for a while. Then Louise sprang to her feet. There was something sparkling between the trees a long way off – water!

'Tim, come on! I think I know where we are!'

She grabbed his hand and together they ran through the trees. It *was* water! The Sound!

And there, much further on, they could see towers...

She was stumbling over her words, but at last she managed to explain: 'I know that view, it looks almost exactly like the one from the window in Mrs Rahbek's sitting-room, so it can't be far to Hill

House, where they can tell us the best way into town
– that's Copenhagen over there, with the towers!'

Chapter Six

They were packing up in an instant, but not quickly
enough to prevent Louise from remembering a new
problem: Mr and Mrs Rahbek knew perfectly well
that she was Danish, and though Tim could speak
only a few words of Danish – and even they sounded
pretty comical – she had discovered long since that
he understood a great deal. And the first person they
would ask about at Hill House would be 'Uncle
Drewsen' and, worse still, *Grandfather*. Tim knew
that word; in the houses where there had been a man
at home it had always been a grandfather, because
the others had gone into Copenhagen. Tim would
discover that she had been deceiving him.

If only she had told him everything long ago! But
that was what came of being a coward: she had
wanted to tell him, in fact there was no reason not to
tell him, because Tim was not an enemy, nor an
Englishman, nor anything but *Tim*, the person she
knew best in all the world, the only person she had

entirely to herself, to whom she was Louise and not merely 'one of the children'.

The trouble was that the right moment had never come, and she had gradually stopped thinking about it at all. But now – she could not possibly say it now! If she were to tell him now, Tim would think it was because she had to, in order not to be unmasked. Perhaps he would never believe she had come to feel it was so unimportant that she did not even remember it.

Louise bit her lip. What on earth was she to do?

It was Tim who quite unwittingly saved her from her dilemma. They had almost reached Hill House when he stopped his horse, Lasse, under a tree.

'Louise, I've been thinking,' he said slowly. 'I really am not too keen on lying to someone you know – shall I wait here? You're not afraid of the dark, you could walk that little distance quite quickly, while I stay with the horses. I'll be able to hear you if you call.'

'Yes, and it will be quicker, too,' said Louise eagerly. 'I was just wondering what would happen if the doors are locked. I think I'll go to the kitchen door and see if Stine is there. If I just stay outside she certainly won't be able to recognize me.'

'And that means we'll be able to avoid upsetting her – the lady – too,' Tim went on. 'I had completely forgotten that your clothes are so unsuitable.'

Although, he thought, as she ran down to the house ahead of him in the dark, she did not look much like a boy, either. Not even in the dark. But of course, no one would dream that a girl might be going around in boy's trousers.

He had just taken an apple out of his pocket when he heard voices from the house – men's voices – *English* voices!

He flung the reins over the lowest branch of the tree and set off at a run. 'Where do you think you're going, you little rascal?' said one voice. And then Louise: 'Let me go, you...you...I want to speak to Mrs Rahbek. Ow, you *beast*!'

There was no time to think that this was exactly what was meant not to happen – someone had caught Louise!

He had struck the man's arm before he even realized that he was holding the riding crop in his hand. 'Let go of my little brother at once, sir!' he said sternly.

'What the devil...' The men turned in surprise and the one who had been holding Louise let her go in sheer astonishment.

They were ordinary soldiers.

Tim put his arm round Louise's shoulders and pushed her back a little. 'Where is your officer? What has happened to the people in the house?'

The soldiers looked at one another and one of

76

them scratched the back of his neck. 'The colonel is having dinner, sir,' he said sheepishly. 'We're billeted here. I don't know anything about the owners.'

'Then you'd better announce me to the colonel,' said Tim. 'The name is Brandon – Timothy Brandon, of Brandon Hall.'

Louise held her breath, but the soldier said, 'Yes, sir,' obediently, and even bowed before he turned and went into the house.

His companions took a few steps back, and Louise whispered anxiously: 'But, Tim, if they find the letter...'

Tim held his ground calmly, without even looking at her. 'You're my younger brother, remember that. Look stupid, if you can, and leave me to do the talking.'

The soldier came back and took them to the house, where an officer was eating at the table in Mrs Rahbek's own sitting-room. He looked up when Louise and Tim came in. 'Well?' he said.

Tim took a step into the room and bowed politely. 'I'm Timothy Brandon, sir. We have come to visit the people who live here, a Mr and Mrs Rahbek, sir.'

'Yes, they're in the town with their family, I believe. My name is Sheridan. What are you two boys doing here? Where do you come from?'

Tim said that they had been visiting their Aunt Isabel in Elsinore.

The colonel's eyes narrowed. 'Quite a step in the wrong direction, eh, Tim?'

'Well, you see, sir...' Tim hesitated and the colonel interrupted him. 'Took a detour to see the fun, eh?'

But he did not seem annoyed. Tim gave a lopsided smile and said: 'Well, sir...'

And then of course the colonel had to say just what Tim had been expecting: he 'could not be responsible for letting a couple of boys wander about as things were now', and they must stay here overnight and wait until he could see an opportunity of getting them back on the right road to Elsinore.

'But, sir...' Tim began.

The colonel had been looking friendly enough until now, but at once his face became stern. 'No nonsense, Tim! You're quite old enough to know that I can't do anything else. In any case, I promise you that if this business goes wrong, as it very well may, you'll soon stop finding it exciting!'

'But it hasn't gone wrong yet, sir?' asked Tim anxiously – 'I mean, war hasn't been declared or anything?'

'No, we're still negotiating ... but it seems rather hopeless...'

The colonel then offered them both something to eat and when they said they had eaten already he led them through the large drawing-room and unlocked the door to a room which Louise knew to be Mr Rahbek's study.

'No messing about, now!' he said sternly. 'We'll keep you locked up in here because I've no other place to put you. You can take down a book to read if you treat it properly. This is the home of a civilized and scholarly gentleman, and we must behave with proper decency – in this house, at least.'

Then he said good night and locked the door behind him.

'Phew!' said Tim, when he had gone. 'Oh well, it might have been worse. The question is now, how are we to get away again? We shall have to wait until Colonel Sheridan has gone to bed then we can easily get out of the windows.'

'But, Tim,' Louise objected, 'if the colonel thinks it's bedtime, that means the gate will be locked.'

Tim asked what gate she was talking about and Louise looked at him in amazement. 'Copenhagen is a fortified town, Tim! There is a moat right round the town and on the bridges there are gates that are locked every night.'

'Do you mean they turn the key on the town every night, like a town in a fairy tale?' asked Tim incredulously. 'Does the king go round with his crown on his head, locking the gates himself?'

Louise giggled. 'Idiot! The king is insane, and the

Crown Prince isn't here, is he? But all the same, the gates are locked every night and unlocked in the morning by the person whose job it is. If only I knew what time they locked up...'

Tim said in that case they would simply have to stay here overnight, there was nothing else for it. They were already arranging the mattresses the colonel had given them, when they heard voices close by.

'Holse – tell me...' – they could hear every word through the wall – '... do you know someone called Brandon? That was the boys' name, remember? There's something odd about this: they are the children of well-bred parents, and of course it's not surprising that they should have family here, there's more than one English family in Elsinore, I know, and people being as nervous as they are at home, it sounds quite reasonable that worried parents should send their children out of the country for fear of invasion...'

'Yes, so what's funny about it?' asked the other voice.

'Simply that one of the boys is a girl,' said Colonel Sheridan. 'It's all very well for a couple of boys to go off on an adventure, believing that war is one big game, but this Tim comes from a good family and seems like a bright, sensible boy, too. I think it's pretty odd that he should put his little sister into boy's clothes and take her along on an adventure in the present circumstances. He knew well enough what was going on, and from what Jenkins told me he was both authoritative and effective when he came to help her – and quick as light, too!'

Tim and Louise both heard something about 'looking into it in the morning' before the voices faded from the next-door room.

They looked at each other in silence.

'How does he know I'm a girl?' whispered the startled Louise.

Tim gave his lopsided smile. 'You bobbed when you said good night. I hoped he hadn't noticed.'

How could she have done something so stupid! The relief when she had discovered where they were – the panic when the soldiers suddenly appeared out of the dusk, and her fright that they might do something to Tim, before she saw they were listening to him just as if he were a grown-up – it was all suddenly too much. There was nothing she could do to stop the tears that welled up in her eyes and spilled down her cheeks.

'You simply mustn't howl,' begged Tim, handing over a rather grubby handkerchief. 'You're usually so brave. I think I'd probably have bowed, if I'd been wearing girl's clothes – it's not the kind of thing you think of in the heat of the moment.'

Louise dried her eyes and managed to produce a

little smile. The thought of Tim in girl's clothes was too much!

'But that means we've got to go tonight,' Tim went on, 'whether the town gates are locked or not. Colonel Sheridan seemed pleasant enough, but that other one, Holse, we haven't seen yet, and I simply *can't* risk anything, Louise, for Uncle Arthur's sake. And if we tear up the letter...'

'Yes, of course,' said Louise calmly. 'We'll get going when they've gone to sleep.'

The greatest problem had been not to fall asleep themselves, but then they began reading to each other out of one of Shakespeare's plays from Mr Rahbek's bookshelves; it was something about some very stupid artisans who were going to take part in a play and kept on muddling up their lines. Louise and Tim took turns reading the parts and were laughing so hard that it was lucky there was a room between them and the two officers.

In the end there was silence throughout the house and outside. The window was no problem. The little squeak it gave when Tim cautiously began to open it was quickly dealt with by rubbing the latch with a candle. Louise crawled ahead under the windows, along the side of the house, but it took them a heart-thumping eternity to crawl quietly enough not to wake up Colonel Sheridan and the other officer inside. Louise's plan was that they should steal down through Mrs Rahbek's garden and out through a gap she knew was there. That way they could get right out of the grounds, because there would obviously be at least one or two soldiers on guard outside.

At last they dared to straighten up.

'Now it's just a question of whether Lasse and Lise are where I left them,' whispered Tim. 'I had to throw the reins over a branch in a hurry. They'll be glad to see us, if they're there, so the first thing we must do is hold their muzzles before they can whinny...'

This went according to plan, as if the two horses understood that it was important for them to be quiet.

'Walking pace,' Tim warned, still whispering, when they were in the saddle. 'It would be nice to gallop, but we'll make less noise walking.' For, sure enough, there had been a couple of men on guard at the bottom of the garden, easily visible in silhouette against their little watch-fire.

Louise had the feeling that her heart was thumping right up to her ears; it was almost more than she could do to ride so slowly, and Tim seemed to be intent on riding crosswise, she thought, so they were not getting very far away from the house.

She was right: that was what he was doing. We still have the cover of the trees, he was thinking worriedly, but they stop over there – and I can't see

83

any other way back to our road than across that bright, open stretch.

'If anyone shouts, we don't stop,' he said, trying to sound perfectly calm. 'All we can do is to speed up. Keep close beside me.'

Louise nodded.

Now they had reached the open stretch, and of course it had to be a clear, starlit night, too! Just then Lasse whinnied impatiently.

'Halt! Who goes there?'

'Lean forward, and we'll make a dash for it!' said Tim, giving Lasse a slap.

They had almost crossed the little clearing when they heard a bang. Both horses whinnied in terror and began to rear and Tim said something that Louise could not hear. She got Lise down on all fours again and gave him a quick look.

'Ride, confound it! I've been hit...*ride*, Louise! I can manage!'

Afterwards Louise did not know how she had done it. Tim had only one slack hand on the reins – the other was holding his shoulder – perhaps it was because of that, and because they had been riding so close together, that she could grab Tim's reins and force both horses into a trot.

'Hold on!' she hissed furiously. 'We're across – now!'

Once they were in the shelter of a tall copse, she

pulled both horses up. Tim was swaying in the saddle. 'Tim! they've got to get their horses out first – there *is* time, if you could manage to scramble over in front of me.'

Tim would have protested, but he was much too tired, and there was a strange mist in front of his eyes. In a moment he would probably fall off his horse, and it would be just like her to dismount and start bandaging him up, so they could easily be caught and taken back, the two of them, with no trouble to anyone.

'Gently... gently... Lasse, Lise, quietly now! Close together, so that Tim can get across...' Her voice was so soft and low, one would never have believed it was the same voice that had hissed at him a moment ago. And over he came, one way or another; but he ended up lying exhausted across the horse, like a pig for the slaughter. 'You're off your head,' he muttered feebly. 'What are you going to do now?'

As soon as he was on her horse, Louise had them trotting again.

'I think I can find the place where Stine lives – I *think* I can. She's a farm woman who takes letters and packets in for Mrs Rahbek when she goes to Copenhagen. It's not very far, Tim, and I know she'll help us. Can you make it? Tim! You're not dead, are you?'

Tim mumbled something, but the only word she

could hear was 'crazy'. That must be me, she thought irritably. It helped to feel irritated. Stupid boy! He probably thinks I ought to let him paddle his own canoe – boys always think they're the only ones who can do anything. There should be a hawthorn bush over by the henyard – and that dog which barked like a mad thing – what was his name, now? Tim and his uncle and their bombs and ... and, I think we're there...

There certainly was a dog, barking like mad. Karo! His name was Karo. Louise called softly to him and he stopped barking, barked again, Louise called again – and the door opened.

'Oh, Lordie, what an ungodly sight ... it is the Englishmen coming, is it? Lordie, Lordie – at this time of night!'

It was Stine. Louise almost swooned from sheer relief. Then she pulled herself together.

'Stine, it's only me, Louise, come over from the Drewsens.'

'Glory be, child! What are you doing here? And in the middle of the night, too? And what is that you've got with you, Miss Louise?'

Suddenly Louise was desperately tired. 'It's a boy,' she said simply. 'We know him. They shot at us from Hill House when we didn't stop.'

Suddenly the good woman seemed to turn into someone quite different, not in the least respectful, even if she was always saying 'Miss Louise' and 'the young gentleman'. Now she was just like Dolly at home when something was amiss. She lifted Tim down as if he were a sack of particularly fine apples which must not be bruised, and carried him into the house, into a small room which contained two beds and a chair and washstand.

'Now we'll just put the young gentleman on the bed, while I get a little warm milk for you, Miss Louise,' she said firmly. 'He's passed out, so he won't know anything, but we've got to have you on your feet, Miss Louise, because you'll have to help me get his coat off so we can bandage him up.'

The warm milk helped a lot, and so did Stine's comment that it looked as if the bullet had passed cleanly through Tim's shoulder. 'He's fainted because of all the blood pouring out,' she said. 'He'll come to again, and if you'll help, Miss Louise, we'll get that wound tied up tight!'

So it was no good turning faint. Louise clenched her teeth, and soon Tim was lying well bandaged in the clean bed, and Stine was in the kitchen finding something for him to drink.

As soon as she had shut the door Tim opened his eyes.

'Well, you found her,' he said. 'You shouldn't have looked at all that blood, you silly!' It would have sounded terribly arrogant, if his voice had not trembled a little. 'But I didn't say anything, you see, so that I wouldn't have to speak English. What was that stuff she put on my shoulder first?'

'Some powdered basil. And did you also understand that the bullet went straight through?'

'Yes, that's good, then we won't need a doctor. Will you be allowed to stay in here?'

Louise said that was for her to decide, and Tim smiled weakly. Oh, Louise!

Stine came back, with something hot which tasted simply disgusting and which she called camomile and camphor drops, and then he was suddenly so tired and so sleepy that he knew nothing.

Louise had been prepared to insist on having her own way if Stine had wanted her to sleep somewhere else, but Stine did not seem to have the kind of ideas that other grown-ups thought so important whenever there was a question of being 'proper'. She simply shook her head as she took both Tim's and Louise's clothes, saying that they needed a wash. 'And you must sleep now, too, Miss Louise,' she said. 'There will be time to talk tomorrow.'

Time was just what they did not have, but Louise was too exhausted to worry any more. She lay down on the clean, neat bed, which smelled faintly of lavender, and fell asleep as soon as her head touched the pillow.

Chapter Seven

For a moment Louise did not know what had woken her, and another moment passed before she remembered where they were; it was possible to make out vague outlines in the little room, but it was still night-time, and dark outside, so she could not have slept so very long.

The letter! Tim had fallen asleep before she could tell him that she had seen her chance to fish Uncle Arthur's letter out of Tim's trouser pocket before Stine had taken their clothes away – what if he were to wake up now and discover its loss! After all, he still believed that she was English. Suddenly she could not bear it a moment longer. She had to tell him she was Danish.

He was breathing rather strangely; perhaps he needed to have his pillows rearranged to make him comfortable – then it wasn't really waking him up – even if she *did* wake him!

She slipped cautiously out of her bed and over to

his. 'Tim,' she whispered, 'you're not comfortable, you're breathing so loudly.'

Something that hurt him was hurting even more, and there was someone who wanted him to do something or other – if only it was not so difficult to open his eyes! 'Louise,' he murmured painfully.

'Sssh!'

He tried to sit up, but fell back on the pillows with a little gasp. 'Is there something wrong? Nothing has happened to you, has it?'

'No, no, just lie still, as long as you can stay awake for a moment. Tim, I just wanted to tell you that I took Uncle Arthur's letter before Stine went off with our clothes ... and ... and that I'm not English, I'm Danish...'

'Yes, I know that,' Tim's tired voice whispered.

'You *know*!' Louise was so annoyed that she almost forgot to whisper. 'How long have you known? And why didn't you say? I was so worried when I began to think about it last night...'

Tim smiled weakly. 'It was probably the same as it was for you: I had forgotten all about it, and I wasn't absolutely sure until I heard Stine talking about your grandfather. The old gentleman out at the mill is your grandfather, isn't he?'

Louise nodded in the darkness.

'Aren't you at all cross with me?' she asked, scarcely able to believe it.

'I can't see it really matters. I mean, at first there was no reason for you to say anything about it, and then Uncle Arthur came, and – well, you probably thought at first that it was better to say nothing, and then you forgot about it, didn't you? And I didn't think about it, either, until you ran into those soldiers this evening. It really doesn't matter what you are, because you're still Louise, aren't you? Phew, it's so hot...'

Louise put her hand on his forehead as she had seen her Aunt Philla do to little Michael when he had measles. It was fiery hot and dripping wet!

'Stine warmed some milk – what if I raised you carefully with the pillow and put the cup in your right hand?'

It still hurt badly, but the milk was good, and cooling, as was Louise's hand on his forehead.

'Do you understand everything?' she whispered, wonderingly.

'Of course I don't,' Tim whispered back. 'I'm only a boy, aren't I? But I do know you, at any rate. You are Louise and you wake me up in the middle of the night when I'm fast asleep! Thanks for the milk.'

The last word was scarcely out before he was asleep again, but Louise lay awake for a long time. There was so much gratitude inside her that she thought she would surely burst. Tim understood all about it, and he thought it didn't matter at all who was English and who was Danish, as long as they knew each other, and most of all as long as they were Tim and Louise.

Oh, yes! But he had certainly remembered, when he heard the soldier grab her, and rushed in to save her, with that dangerous letter in his pocket – and that was before they knew that Colonel Sheridan was quite nice!

If only he were better tomorrow... Louise did not fall asleep again until the sky was almost light.

But Tim was not better the next day: on the contrary. Stine took one look at him when she came in with their clothes, quite clean again, and freshly ironed, then she said that there was no question of his getting up that day, because anyone could see that the young gentleman had a high temperature. 'But I don't know where to get a doctor,' she said anxiously. 'Copenhagen is completely shut off and there are Englishmen around everywhere here. Oh Lord, what a responsibility, what would Madam say, and why were you wearing boy's clothes, Miss Louise? I've never heard the like...'

Louise said they *must* get into Copenhagen and they had thought it would be better if she were dressed as a boy. Stine nodded thoughtfully. 'Well, well,' she said, 'that may be so. But you can't go into Copenhagen today, and you will have to help me change the bandage, Miss Louise, so that we can see to the wound, and you'll have to promise me to stay in here. I dare not think what Madam would say, and the family at the Mill, if anything happened to you, Miss Louise – they say the Englishmen just go on advancing, without anyone doing anything to stop them.'

And that was how it was that day and the next day, Louise thought. Every morning and evening she helped Stine to dress the wound with spirit and sprinkle it with powdered herbs before putting on a clean bandage. The first day was the worst, because Tim had been completely confused and feverish in the brief moments when he was awake. Stine's face had taken on a very startled expression, and Louise had suddenly realized that the words he muttered when they touched him were in English. Fortunately Stine did not seem to think there was anything odd about Louise's hasty explanation that it was because he had a tutor at home who was English. 'Lots of people have them at home in St Croix,' she said, adding that anyway his mother was English – there were lots of English people at home. 'A lot of people like Tim don't even speak Danish properly, so you mustn't be surprised, Stine, if he says something odd.'

All Stine had said was 'Well, I'm blessed!' and if Louise had not been so frightened she would certainly have giggled; from Stine's tone of voice one could tell that she was deeply sorry for those poor folks who had to put up with talking foreign! But on that terrible first day she could think of nothing but Tim, dripping with sweat and rolling his head on the pillow as he muttered broken, garbled phrases. He scarcely opened his eyes when they tried to make him drink a little, and that was almost worse, because he clearly had no idea who they were, even when he was staring straight at them with blank, brilliant eyes.

All the same, he had thanked them politely, in Danish, that evening, when Stine had lifted him up while Louise held the mug for him to drink some soup.

She scarcely slept at all that night, afraid that Tim might stop breathing while she was asleep, and in the morning he was lying so still and white that she had been quite certain he was going to die. At least it was a good thing that he was too ill to hear her, because she had been in such despair that she had knelt beside his bed and clasped his hand between hers while she pleaded and begged with him and with God not to let him die – and all the time perhaps she was only thinking of herself ... Life would not have been worth living if Tim were no longer there – the one person who understood everything so well and knew that she was Louise and not just 'one of the children'. It would have made her sound terribly feeble if anyone had heard, and Tim disliked it when she cried...

But during the morning she could see that he was a little better, and he recognized her, too, so they could talk to each other, even if he got tired very quickly and had to sleep again.

He himself was very annoyed about it all, and grumbled at himself for being so spineless that he could only just stand up if Stine helped him.

He had lost a lot of blood, Stine said, and there had been a great danger of inflammation in the wound; that was why he was so weak.

Louise did not care. Everything that had happened before was so far away – now there was only Stine's clean little whitewashed room, and Stine herself, taking such good care of Tim and bringing him food which he could drink, though it was still proper food, with milk, soup, fruit juice, egg-yolk and other good things. They would have to leave, of course, as soon as he was well enough, but meanwhile it was safe and nice here, with Tim, and all the things they had to talk about. Louise told him about her homes in St Croix and at the Mill and he told her what things were like in England. You could tell Tim why it felt so – *lonely*, when you were just one of so many children all the time, so that only Dolly, and Miss Gertrude at the Mill, always remembered your name and did not get it mixed up. And even they did not understand what was going on in your head.

Tim said it had nothing to do with there being too many children: he had only two big sisters and a grown-up brother, who had always been away, first at Eton and then at Oxford, because in England only little boys, and girls, of course, had lessons at home. That could feel lonely too.

'But now you've got me,' he said firmly. 'That is, if only I can get on my feet again. Have you kept count of what day it is now?'

Louise had just told him that it had been Sunday the day before yesterday, when Stine came in with lunch.

'Today the young gentleman could eat a little chicken,' she said. 'It's good, with fine green vegetables in the sauce, and I made it with cream – yes, we've still got food to put in our mouths, but, oh Lord, everything else is upside down! Now they're actually burning the ropewalks in there!'

Tim put down his fork. 'Who are?' he asked.

Stine said no one could tell. 'Some say it's the Englishmen, others think it's our own fellows, but that sounds too silly, to my way of thinking. And you mustn't stop eating, young gentleman! I think it must have been the Englishmen, some say they're savages who go around without trousers, so what can you expect? But you mustn't be frightened, Miss Louise, no Englishman in skirts is coming here, Stine

96

will see to that; we'll set our Karo on them if they come, bare bottoms are just right for him to bite into, you'll see!' With another reminder to Tim to eat up his good food, she left the room, still shaking her head, and Tim, who had gone bright red in the face, covered his mouth and shook with laughter.

'Sssh! Tim!'

'I'm laughing as quietly as I can,' he hiccuped. 'Louise... oh, no! Trouserless wild men in skirts!'

Louise was explaining patiently that Stine must have misheard, because they only existed on the Danish coat of arms, and they most certainly did not wear skirts, when Tim collapsed again. 'They are Scots!' he moaned. 'There must be a Scottish regiment somewhere near – trouserless savages! Just wait till my cousin James hears that description of his precious kilt!'

And then it was Louise's turn to snatch up a pillow and bury her face in it.

Tim watched her with delight: it was a long time since she had laughed until the dimples deepened in her cheeks. He took a good mouthful of food and when it had been chewed sufficiently and Louise had stopped giggling he asked if she knew what the ropewalks were.

She shook her head. 'Perhaps they make rope there, but surely it can't be the Danes who are burning them, can it?'

Tim said, on the contrary, they should have done it long ago. 'With a fortified town, the whole point is to leave open land all round it, so that you can sit there comfortably and fire on the enemy as he advances,' he explained. 'When Stine has gone to bed you must help me to get on my feet; it's high time we went, and now that I can eat proper food, I must surely be able to walk as well!'

He was a little wobbly still, but he was managing to walk gingerly once or twice round the little room and the next morning he went on pestering Stine until she helped him into his clothes and gave him permission to sit outside with Louise for a while behind the little house, in the noonday sun. Louise was a little surprised that he obediently kept the arm with the wounded shoulder in the sling all the time, because he himself said it did not hurt any more, and he was eating as if he had been starving for months!

Tim knew that he was eating against time – not because he was particularly hungry – and he kept his arm in its sling, even though it was difficult to remember, because he must gather his strength quickly and let his shoulder heal well before they could get away. They had to get through those gates before his countrymen reached them, and from Stine's chatter it was clear that there was still no one who would put the slightest obstacle in their path.

She was full of stories, this good Stine, and though

both Tim and Louise realized that they should not rely too greatly on any of them, they could not help wondering.

'I think it sounds like a very peculiar war,' said Louise thoughtfully, sniffing at a rose she had picked. 'We know it's going on, but it's as if both the Danes and the English are waiting for the others to begin the fighting, isn't it? And the way Stine talks, it's almost as if she's read all those dreadful things in an exciting book and doesn't really believe in her heart of hearts that they're true. And yet they *must* be, because Colonel Sheridan did push Mr and Mrs Rahbek out of Hill House, even if he did it politely, and if it's true that there are masses of English soldiers on the road to Frederiksberg; it's not so far from there to the West Gate...'

'We must leave tomorrow,' said Tim determinedly. 'How will Stine take it? She doesn't even understand what I'm saying.'

'No, but she does understand me!' Louise straightened up on the seat. 'If you can make a soldier listen to you and even call you 'Sir', I must be able to be just as firm with our dear Stine.'

Tim thought to himself that it would not be easy to find anything that looked less 'firm' than Louise, sitting there in her cousin's trousers, with the sunshine on her curls, and playing with a rose which was bigger than her slightly bronzed little hand!

Aloud he said that at least they must give the kind woman some money: 'All those eggs and good things she's used on us, and she's been feeding Lise and Lasse as well, and hiding them so that they wouldn't be requisitioned by some passing volunteer – and she must be quite poor, isn't she?'

Poverty was something else she knew nothing about, Louise thought, ashamed. But Stine was always happy, and she had food and a house to live in as well – was that being poor? In that case it was surely not as bad as the things you read about in books. But it was like Tim to think of it.

Tim himself was not particularly happy when they said goodbye to Stine the next morning. She had wrung her hands and begged them to stay. In the end she had plucked up her courage and tried to give them orders – and what chance had he to be listened to, when he could not even speak the wretched language correctly? But there stood Louise, suddenly as straight and strong as a little willow tree. 'You must be quiet now, Stine,' she had said, gravely. 'You have been so good to us – I would never have managed Tim's shoulder alone, and we are both grateful. But you must understand that it's important we should reach my uncle in the town before it is too late. Tim is used to looking after me and you have no authority over either him or me, Stine, and my uncle will understand that too, when I tell him what great care you took of us!'

Stine had sniffed a little and said, 'Lord, Lord,' and helped them both into their saddles. Then she had tied a great parcel of food to Tim's saddle and sniffed again, and said, 'God keep you, Miss Louise, and the young gentleman!' and stood watching them and waving until they were out of sight.

And once again it had been Louise who had managed and got them away safely. And what had he ever done?

He tried to stammer out some of this, but Louise interrupted him: 'Yes, and I suppose it was me who had that letter in my pocket, when I flew at a bunch of soldiers and risked being shot as a spy or something just to save you, wasn't it? And of course it was you who was stupid enough to curtsey to Colonel Sheridan and make him suspicious so that we had to fly for our lives and be shot at?'

Tim felt a little comforted, but had to admit that the idea of being taken for a traitor had simply never entered his head that evening — 'at least, not until I got down to where you were!'

Chapter Eight

The weather was beautiful, and it was good to be out again, riding along peacefully side by side. It was pretty here, too, Tim thought, with all this greenery, and the towers and church spires in the distance where Copenhagen lay.

People were busy on their farms, as if everything were perfectly normal and ordinary— ... but this thought had barely entered his head before he heard shots in the distance; out of the corner of his eye he saw Louise jump, but she simply patted Lise's neck without speaking and rode on.

'It was a long way off,' said Tim reassuringly, and Louise nodded and gave him a little smile, but her eyes were very dark.

'If you get really frightened, you must tell me. You mustn't do more than you dare – perhaps I can practise a few phrases of Danish until they sound right, so that you don't need to come right into the town.'

Louise just shook her head and said, almost as if she had not been listening: 'I was thinking – I have no idea where to find this Mr Bartholin whose house my uncle and aunts are living in.'

Oh no! Wandering about in a besieged capital (even if it did not look very big from here), and asking for someone, when you did not even know where he lived!

'Perhaps there's someone else whose address you know?' asked Tim, trying to sound practical and undismayed.

'Yes, there is Brewer's Court, Bryggergaard, where Mrs Rahbek's father lives. His name is Heger and I think the street is called North Street – Nørregade in Danish. Stine thought that was where Mrs Rahbek had gone.'

'All right then, we'll try there,' said Tim cheerfully. 'I'm hungry, aren't you?'

It was mostly to give himself time to think, but there was no doubt that a little food slipped down quite well. Where was that avenue, where Stine had said there were English soldiers? It would certainly not be a good idea to go barging straight into them. Louise said all she knew was that it was straight ahead, which Tim did not find very reassuring. At that moment he caught sight of a boy a little way off. 'Couldn't you ask him?' he suggested, hastily tying the cloth round his neck.

103

Louise called the boy and he eagerly accepted the offer of a little food. His name was Frederik and he chatted away merrily as he munched. It was terrifically exciting in the town, he said. 'Everyone is doing something, hospitals are being organized with black flags on them so you can find them, and some people are cleaning out old wells, and the fire service is helping to set up guard-posts everywhere and tell people what to do when the Englishmen go into the attack, putting out fires and so forth, and people are *hauling* food and wine up to our soldiers on the ramparts – a little too much, my stepfather says, but of course everybody wants to do something.'

Then his eagerness dwindled. 'I'm not allowed to do anything. I could handle a carbine, I'm twelve, and Fritz is only fourteen and he's been allowed to go in with his father; he shoots very well, almost as well as one of the squire's gamekeepers. I live with my mother and stepfather, you see, because my father's dead. Oh, you should just see the riflemen's horses! They're waiting in our street. Only today I was thinking I would like to go and have a look at the Englishmen out here, but there's so much to do in the town! We've been let off school so we've got the whole day to watch the soldiers drilling, the militia and the lifeguards, and the student corps. But the fifteen *rigsdaler* soldiers are absolutely pathetic, they haven't got uniforms or anything, and they're scared, too. But my stepfather says it's not right to laugh at them, they're doing their best.'

'What's your stepfather's name?' asked Louise curiously. 'Is he nice?'

Frederik said oh, yes, and that his name was Benzon and he was the supervisor at Count Schimmelmann's sugar refinery, and then he went on with his enthusiastic account of everything there was to see in Copenhagen. 'Old Bishop Balle is marching round the ramparts in a big wig without a hat and comforting people if he can get them to listen to him, and Knudsen, the actor, is singing patriotic songs and people sing along with him and everything is great fun.'

Tim and Louise looked at each other.

'But isn't anyone frightened?' said Louise, looking at the strange boy in amazement.

'No, what an idea!' Frederik licked a greasy finger contentedly. 'Let them come! We're just waiting to thrash them, but they've got to start it, because war hasn't been declared and General Peymann says that means it's not correct to fire on them. Well, I must be getting on. Thanks for the food!'

And he was off, whistling cheerfully.

'What an idiot!' said Tim disapprovingly. 'Did he say we should turn off to the left?'

'Yes, soon, behind something called the Shooting Galleries, but, Tim, we must remember that we're the only ones who know anything about the rockets, and if everyone in Copenhagen just thinks it's so exciting, then there's nothing wrong with him thinking so, too.'

'No, of course not,' said Tim quickly. What an idiot he was, criticizing, and forcing her to defend her fellow-countrymen to him.

Louise gave him a searching look and asked how his shoulder was getting on, and Tim said it was fine and they had better get through this West Gate while it was still open.

'Do you think the English are as close as that?' Louise did her best not to sound scared. Tim said that if Frederik had come through only a little earlier, then of course they could as well.

But it took time to make the detour, and all the time they had to ask the way, so the sun was setting when they reached the gate.

Once they were through, Louise studied Tim's face again. 'We're stopping here,' she said firmly. 'You're tired now, and it looks nice down here, come on, we can find nothing in the dark, anyway.'

Tim was all ready to protest, but realized she was right, and here behind the barrier just inside the gate there were both trees for Lise and Lasse and a seat for themselves.

Kirsebaergangen, Cherry Walk, was the name of the

place, and they got some sleep there, too, although it was late before people stopped strolling past on their evening walk.

But the next morning brought a nasty surprise: Tim woke up, a little stiff and sore in the shoulder, and a little confused, too, until he remembered where they were. Louise was still sleeping comfortably beside him, but – there was no sign of Lise and Lasse! He knew they had been properly tied up, and yet they had gone, and they belonged to Uncle Arthur, or rather, to Lord Cathcart.

Louise, when she woke up, was more worried about the horses themselves. 'Someone has requi... whatever it's called, them while we were asleep. Stine talked about that, Tim, and it's lucky we got inside the ramparts, because it can't be far to walk now. If only they've been taken by someone who'll be good to them!'

In any case it was no good worrying, and Tim hastened to suggest breakfast before she had time to realize that the horses would most probably be used for fighting and might easily get shot.

They were arguing about whether it was Friday or Saturday when they heard music nearby. Louise listened: 'It's on the other side of the gate,' she said with relief. 'Perhaps they are practising out on those shooting galleries that Frederik talked about.'

Tim got up and began to pack their things, a little

awkwardly because his shoulder was hurting, and Louise hurried to help him. 'Look out for that arm, Tim! Perhaps we should leave the blankets here, because by this evening we shall have found somebody. The music sounds good, doesn't it?'

Tim nodded without speaking. He knew all the tunes, and knew that his own countrymen were approaching, bands playing – it was high time they were gone!

But that was easier said than done, because before they were ready to go the sound of a rhythmic march came from the bridge. Tim pulled Louise close against the wall, under a tree, and listened. Fortunately the orders were given in Danish, and now a flock of children came running along the ramparts, cheering: 'The firemen, the firemen! Now we'll see some fun!' And further away, grown-ups were rushing to the spot, talking eagerly. Tim and Louise stayed where they were and as the crowd came closer they could hear a few phrases: 'They say the fleet will attack by the old Pesthouse,' and 'Let's go to Langebro, there'll be plenty to see there.'

'No, wait,' shouted one woman: 'They say the Fire Corps is advancing to stop the Englishmen – yes, look! Fire!'

More and more people were pouring to the spot. 'I think it's the mill at Egypt. No, you can see it's Glaciholm.' 'And there, Eytin is burning too!'

'Oh, thank goodness, the suburbs are on fire now!'

Tim looked at Louise, who stood silently, her eyes very dark. 'What is burning?'

'I don't know,' she whispered. 'It sounds as if it's some farms, real places, where people live, and horses, and dogs and chickens. How can people be glad to see something burning? And why are the Danes burning their own houses? Or letting the firemen do it?'

'They think it's necessary,' said Tim. 'I think it's a silly idea, because I think it's too late. There's nothing we can do about it, Louise. We had better get on with the one thing we *may* be able to do something about. Leave the rugs, they're too heavy to take with us.'

He took her hand and together they walked up to the gate and continued into the town. Shots could be heard at regular intervals, but they were quite a long way off. 'I think we should try to head for those two towers,' said Louise. 'If I remember rightly, Nørregade is near there. The people at Bryggergaarden, Brewer's Court, must know where Uncle Drewsen is.'

Tim was happy to get away from the ramparts: people were walking there as if they were out for a Sunday stroll, in and out among the soldiers; but they were the most unruly collection of soldiers Tim had ever seen! Some lay dozing or chatting round the cannon, some were practising on their musical instruments, and now and then a trooper came galloping along at top speed in spite of all the pedestrians wandering about. In one place a whole pyramid of guns had been stacked up while their owners stood in a queue at stalls where women were selling bread or drinks. And to judge by the way some of them were singing and bawling and laughing, the drinks were the kind that could make them quite tipsy.

Some of them were wearing bits of uniform, others no more than a military cap – except for a few young men in short, dark-blue jackets with a white stripe: students, Louise said. It was lucky that she simply did not understand what was going on, thought Tim anxiously, because if this was Copenhagen's idea of defence, he would not give a bean for the whole town!

It was quieter in the little streets, where almost only women and children were to be seen, but here too everyone seemed to be in high good humour.

'We're getting water,' said one boy of whom they asked the way, explaining the full bucket he could scarcely carry. 'It's very important to have masses of water in the water-carts everywhere, in case there's a fire.'

His name was Thomas. Louise and Tim went with him to the courtyard where he lived, to get

110

something to drink. Over by the gate stood a woman and an old man, wringing out washing, and some children were playing in the middle of the courtyard while their mothers shouted to each other across it from the many small windows.

Tim and Louise looked around – an enormous number of people were living here! There were sixteen rooms in the back building alone, with a family in each, Thomas told them proudly.

'It must be awfully uncomfortable with so many people in such a small space,' said Louise, when they had said goodbye to Thomas. Tim said that they were probably used to it.

'Well, anyway, they were in good spirits. But, Tim, can you understand why all the people are smiling and singing and looking so happy?'

Tim said it must be what his cousin James called 'high battle morale' – 'and that's good. It would be much worse if they were scared in advance, because in that case they would panic as soon as anything happened.'

'I see,' said Louise, comforted, reminding herself that, after all, none of them knew anything about the terrible rockets. They believed they were only going to be besieged. And as long as Tim did not think that Danes were stupid...

Chapter Nine

They had no trouble finding Brewer's Court, because everyone knew where Heger lived, and they found Mrs Rahbek there, as well.

'My dear children!' she exclaimed, when she saw them and recognized Louise. 'I thought you had stayed at the Mill with your grandfather – what are you doing here? And in those clothes...'

They had completely forgotten to agree on their story!

Louise thought at lightning speed. The truth would be best, or at least part of it. She began with the English landing at Vedbaek, that morning an eternity ago, then tried to play for time, thinking of something which would make it likely that her grandfather had let her ride into Copenhagen.

'Better tell the truth, Louise!' said Tim suddenly.

Mrs Rahbek smiled and said she agreed, the truth would be best, and after that it was simple. Mrs Rahbek knew English too, in addition to all the other languages Louise knew she understood, so Tim was able to help her tell their story. Mrs Rahbek did not interrupt them once, and when they had finished she said she thought they had managed very well up to now, and when they had had a cup of chocolate each, she would tell them the way down to Bartholin's. She was glad to hear that Colonel Sheridan had been friendly and that Mr Rahbek's study had been locked up, and she gave a ringing laugh at Stine's description of the Scottish soldiers. But then she grew serious again and said that it was a terribly important mission to entrust to two children. Tim was about to interrupt when she went on to say that she could well understand it was the best Major General Wellesley could do, and since he knew Tim could do it, she would try not to worry too much.

'But I haven't even got anyone to send with you at present,' she said anxiously. 'Captain Rahbek is at the university, on guard with his students – in fact everyone has his post to mind these days, and I daren't leave here myself: my sister is out on an errand, and if anything should happen...'

Louise and Tim assured her that they would certainly be able to find the way themselves and, comforted by hot chocolate inside them and a note in Tim's pocket to guide them, they set off down North Street, past the Church of Our Lady and on to Vimmelskaftet.

This Copenhagen was an attractive town, thought Tim, there were so many trees here, and broad streets that let in the sunshine. But it was the same everywhere: people walking about, greeting acquaintances, or standing round chatting as if everything were completely normal and the town not surrounded by enemy soldiers.

Nikolai Square was easily found – you had only to follow the noise! The square was full of booths where butchers were selling their meat, all calling and shouting; by one booth some young serving-maids had gathered round a curly-haired butcher's lad, who flicked his sharp knife in the sunshine so that it glittered, and gave them a very bloody account of what he would do to the Englishmen if they came.

And from the square ran Admiral's Street, where they should find Uncle Drewsen and Louise's aunts.

Louise was about to go in, when Tim laid a hand on her arm. 'What if your uncle is not at home? I mean, what are your aunts like? Are they sensible, like Mrs Rahbek, or what?'

She should have thought about that before! 'I – Tim, I don't really know them,' she said hesitantly. 'They're nice enough, but there are so many of us, my own little cousins, and Grandfather's children, because he married again after my grandmother died

114

– we're all just "the children" – it's mostly Miss Gertrude who looks after us.'

'It won't do,' said Tim firmly. 'Two aunts and a crowd of children! We'll never get away, I know aunts! We're going to have to write a note, and how in the world can we do that, with a flock of small children all over the place – little ones like that *talk*. Is my Danish good enough for me to go and ask for your uncle while you keep out of sight?'

'Yes, I think so,' said Louise, but before they could agree what Tim was going to say, the problem solved itself.

'Here comes Carl!' whispered Louise, turning away a little. 'He's all right, but a bit lazy and careless. You ask for – for Lieutenant Drewsen, and I'll walk on towards the square.'

If only she had thought to tell him what to say! Louise waited in trepidation for Tim to come back.

'What did you say? Did Carl ask what you wanted?'

Tim smiled cheerfully. 'I said I had a message from Mrs Rahbek. Your uncle is annoyed because he hasn't seen any fighting yet, so he's got leave to go off with something called the Chasseurs. He's out at Emily – no, Amalieborg now. And I found out which way to go, too.'

It was a long way. Louise's legs grew very tired, and Tim put his arm back in the sling Stine had made for him. Louise knew what that meant: his shoulder was hurting, but she said nothing, because Tim would only bite her head off if she asked.

But down at the next big square they both forgot their tiredness. Masses of people were there, walking up and down, or standing listening to a brass band playing outside the Raus Gaard Hotel.

'That is the grandest hotel in the town,' Louise explained, 'but I've no idea why they are giving a concert.'

They learned the answer from a boy who overheard her. 'General Peymann has moved in there,' he explained, 'and that's why all those officers are going in and out. My father says the Englishmen's patience will soon run out, but the general has promised to hold Copenhagen, and after all, we can't just hand over the fleet, can we?'

It was dusk by now, but at last they were quite close to Amalieborg, the four palaces forming a great square, with a gigantic equestrian statue in the middle. 'That's really great,' said Tim, impressed.

Louise's eyes followed his. 'Yes, Uncle Drewsen says it was made by an extremely good sculptor, but it's quite old, it – Tim! There he is!'

Uncle Drewsen was standing on the steps arguing with a crowd of other soldiers outside one of the palaces.

'We'll have to wait a bit,' said Tim, 'until we can

116

get hold of him without having to push through the crowd.'

They moved back until they were in one of the arcades, and approached slowly, as if at random. If only it's not completely dark by the time they stop talking, thought Tim anxiously. We shall never find him in the dark among all those people.

'Listen in to everything you can,' he whispered. 'I don't understand half of it, at this distance.'

Louise nodded.

A little later she whispered: 'That one with the gold on his shoulders is the Chief of Chasseurs. His name is von Holstein. He says they must go to Classen's Gardens to see if the Englishmen have built batteries there – and they must cut down trees and ... and burn houses.'

At the same moment they heard a horse at the gallop and glimpsed a rider who rode to the very foot of the steps before leaping off.

Oh, what now? Tim thought impatiently. There was a muttering among the men of the Chasseurs, but it was no longer possible to see individuals, only the outline of their chief and of the messenger. Then one of them raised his voice: 'The attack is postponed!' – so it must be the commandant: 'A marine has deserted, we can't risk his betraying our plan to the enemy. The attack will start early tomorrow morning instead. You meet at five in the morning.'

117

The Chasseurs poured down the steps, but it was impossible to hear anything more now, and it was hopeless trying to find one individual in the dark. Louise made one attempt, after having peered in all directions in vain – she grabbed a young man by the sleeve and asked for Lieutenant Drewsen, but he said he knew no one of that name.

'No, of course, since your uncle is not normally a Chasseur,' Tim comforted her. 'You mustn't let it upset you. The boy we met in the big square said the Englishmen were beginning to lose patience, not that they had already lost it. It's hopeless trying to find your uncle now, we'll only run into someone who says children should not be out alone in the dark.'

Louise had difficulty in making her voice obey her: they had been so close! 'Then what shall we do now, Tim?' she said despondently.

'We'll find a quiet spot where we can sit down and eat. I'm absolutely starving, and so are you, when you stop to think. And we're so tired that we'll lose heart unless we get a little rest. Then we'll see about finding the way back to the place where your uncle is staying, and take turns to sleep until we can catch him as soon as he comes out of the door.'

The plan might not be ideal – among other things, they now had no blankets to roll up in – but the fact that Tim knew what they ought to do helped a lot, and Louise, feeling comforted, put her hand in his and pretended to herself that she did not have a great, sore blister on her left heel.

It was incredible how much eating helped! They had walked back down to the broad street that actually went by that name, and just opposite them was a kind of ruin, in an open space.

'Perhaps that's St Frederik's Church,' said Louise. 'I've heard about it, if so. It's not a real ruin, it's just that they never finished building it because marble became so expensive.'

But it did have solid steps on which they could sit comfortably and spread the food out between them. The moon gave a little light, and at a church, even if it was only half a church, surely nothing much could happen to them.

'I think I've got a better idea now,' Tim said, while they were packing up their bundle, which had shrunk a good deal. 'That boy we met in the square where the band was playing – didn't he say those Classen's Gardens were outside the East Gate? Why don't we go straight out there, instead of walking all the way back again – it may be shorter. And there weren't really any places near your uncle's where we could lie down and sleep properly.'

Louise thought it was a good idea and it turned out that all they had to do was walk straight along

Broad Street. The old gentleman of whom Louise asked the way said disapprovingly that it was much too late for a couple of lads like them to be about, in these uncertain times, but Louise told him calmly that they lived out there, and had just been in to hear the band and lost their way and now they were on their way home.

It wasn't so very far, after all, especially once Tim had torn off a piece of his handkerchief and folded it neatly inside Louise's left shoe so that her blister came above the edge.

But when they got there, the East Gate was locked.

'You'll have to go down to the North Gate and pay your way out,' called a guard from the ramparts above them – 'unless the young gentlemen would like to come up here instead – we've got plenty of brandy!'

'Say no thanks! Hurry up!' Tim hissed.

Louise called back that they had better hurry over to the North Gate. She grabbed Tim's hand and in a few strides they were in the lee of the ramparts.

'Tim, you're shaking! Do you think you've got a temperature?' said Louise anxiously, stopping in her flight.

'No, I'm just furious,' said Tim shortly. 'What a... what a...'

Louise said what did it matter? The soldier had only been joking. 'But, Tim, what about trying the mill up there? If we can't get out, I mean. There might be some flour sacks we could sleep on.'

There were. And in here they were at least safe from soldiers trying to be funny, thought Tim, when after a good deal of crawling to and fro they found themselves inside at last.

'We're both going to sleep now!' he decided. 'It's much too much of a strain trying to take turns, and I shall wake in time anyway, the way I always do at home when I know we're going hunting or something.'

They were asleep almost before they had settled down, and neither the mice nor the guard being changed outside on the ramparts disturbed them. Tim was the first to wake; he would have liked nothing better than to go on sleeping, but it was growing light, so the gate was bound to open soon.

Louise woke up as she always did – that girl wasn't even grumpy in the morning! When you gave her a little shake she simply opened her eyes and smiled.

And there was something to smile at today: they were as white as clowns, with flour from the sacks they had slept on.

'We can eat later, when we reach Classen's Gardens,' said Louise practically. They brushed each other down as thoroughly as possible and set off.

It took them only ten minutes to reach the

121

gardens, which were as big as a park, with trees and paths and little lakes with artificial islands in them.

'It must have been lovely here,' said Louise sadly, for the gardens were no longer so charming: several gazebos and follies had been burned down, trees felled, seats overturned. Tim looked about him uneasily – that newly dug ditch looked very like a firing trench.

Suddenly he saw something – *somebody* – moving, a little way off.

'We'll stay here, just where we are,' he said, 'between the fence and the bushes, so that we can see them if they come this way.'

He had a feeling that they were closer to his own countrymen than he really liked.

They must have been terribly tired, he thought afterwards, because they had been dozing behind the bushes when a terrific noise woke them up. The park was full of soldiers, and now they were rolling in the cannon! Tim counted them: there were eight. He woke Louise cautiously and said she had better see if she could find her uncle quickly, so that they could get away before anything happened.

Louise looked about her. Uncle Drewsen should be easy to find, in his red uniform jacket, because all the Chasseurs were in green.

Only there were firemen here, too, and Life Guards, and a whole crowd of soldiers shouting in

Norwegian, and – oh, there must be thousands of soldiers here!

'No, no,' said Tim calmly, 'but there are probably one or two thousand of them, and three gunboats out in the Sound are coming closer. Danes,' he added quickly. 'Come on, we'll creep along the outside here.'

Louise peered as hard as she could every time they had an open view, but Uncle Drewsen's red jacket was nowhere to be seen among all the green, and the Chasseurs were still to the fore, already across one broad trench.

Suddenly Tim stopped, giving her arm a tug.

'The ones over there are English! It's no good, Louise! Uncle Arthur would make mincemeat of me if I didn't get you away now!' Quite apart from the fact that he himself would never be able to forget it if Louise were shot, he thought. 'Now, you stay here and I'll zigzag to and fro and find your uncle. I'll ask their officer – he must know him, hang it!'

'No, Tim, no!'

'They don't shoot as low as this, Louise, I'll be all right. Anyway, they haven't started yet.'

At that very moment they saw a soldier support his rifle on a tall tree stump and take aim. Then came the sound of the first shot, and an English soldier clutched at his throat and fell beside the building in the middle of the park.

'Bravo, Drewsen!' called a voice.

Louise gave a gasp and before Tim could look round she was flying down towards the place where the rifleman stood.

Tim dropped everything he was holding and rushed after her, so fast that when a senior officer reached out a hand and stopped her just before she reached the first rifleman, he bumped straight into them both.

'Be off with you!' said the officer brusquely. 'This is no place for children!'

Louise tried to wrench herself free. 'A letter for my Uncle Drewsen — he *must* have it!'

The officer placed himself in front of them, with his back to his soldiers, and waved Tim in behind Louise, so that both were covered. 'I will get it to him, when there is time.'

'But there *isn't* any time!' Louise pressed her hand to her mouth to stop herself bursting into tears.

'Please read it, sir,' said Tim calmly in English, pulling the letter out of his pocket.

Louise's panic vanished like dew in the sun. 'If you do anything to Tim...' she said threateningly.

The officer looked down at her and smiled faintly. 'I don't hurt children, my dear.'

'But now you know Tim is English...'

'I don't hurt *any* children,' said the officer firmly. 'Let us hope the same can be said of the English soldiers. But let me read the letter now.'

The first shot had already been followed by several more, but the officer stood calmly where he was, merely moving Tim and Louise over a little when a bullet landed too close. He frowned. 'You are Timothy Brandon?' he said.

Tim's 'Yes' was drowned by an order in English: 'Cease fire!' Tim raised his head – he knew that voice!

'Get those children away from here! You have five minutes!'

The officer glanced over his shoulder, shouted, 'Cease fire!' himself in Danish and led Tim and Louise a little way up the park towards the gate before he stopped. 'Now tell me, very quickly, what kind of message you have brought.'

'You translate, Louise,' said Tim, and began talking, so calmly and briefly that Louise caught his tone. '...some special, completely new rockets, they have a very long range and are very accurate. They have barbs on them, so that they catch on everything – couldn't you make General Peymann understand?'

Tim stopped, but Louise went on: 'Mr von Holstein, you can't let all those people be bombed and burned. I spoke to Tim's uncle myself...'

'When was that?'

'A good many days ago, when he landed at Vedbaek. He says all the English officers are unwilling, but they will *have* to go ahead unless we lend them our fleet. Can't you do anything?'

The officer looked gravely from her to Tim and back again.

'I can try,' he said, 'and that is all. But you two have done everything you were supposed to and a bit more, and now you must go. My best wishes to your uncle, from the Danish Chief of Chasseurs, Tim, and assure him of my respect. You can say that his nephew has it, too.' He turned and shouted: 'Hauch!'

A very young man ran up and bowed.

'These two are Louise and Tim – and this is Carsten Hauch. Hauch, will you make sure these children get through the gate safely, and away from the ramparts!'

Then he had gone, and only a moment later the roar of the cannon began again.

The young man was obviously not pleased to have been sent away from the park, and as soon as they were inside the gate Tim told him that they could find their own way from there.

Chapter Ten

It was an extraordinary feeling. Louise and Tim walked very slowly back along Broad Street, not even speaking to each other, and when they reached the square of the night before, with the half-finished church, they turned in as if by agreement and sat down on the steps, still without speaking.

'Yes, but we did do it, in the end,' said Louise at last, leaning her head against a column. 'What now, Tim?'

Suddenly Tim wanted to shout and stamp and swear; there was always something to be decided, and unless he happened to be unconscious, it was always he who had to decide what was best. He was sick and tired of it.

Louise gave a little smile at the sight of his set face. 'Well, I think we should eat first, don't you?' It usually helped if Tim had something to eat.

'We haven't got anything,' said Tim sulkily. 'I dropped the package when you bolted down into the

127

thick of it all like a lunatic.'

Louise sighed. 'Oh well – we'll have to go without. Tim, you simply must stop letting people know you're English every time anything happens. If even my own nice Uncle Drewsen starts shooting as soon as he sees anyone… you make me so frightened.'

Tim scowled at her. 'How do you think I feel, when you go tearing out among the bullets at the drop of a hat!'

'Tim, we're quarrelling!' The girl was giggling, for heaven's sake! He could not help grinning himself, and at that moment the boy from yesterday came across the square towards them.

'Hallo,' he said. 'What are you doing here?'

'Nothing,' said Louise quickly and reminded Tim to put his neckcloth on again. 'He can scarcely speak for the pain in his throat,' she explained. 'We got lost yesterday evening – we don't know Copenhagen too well. My name's Louise Drewsen. This is Tim.'

'My name's Steen,' said the boy politely. 'Steen Bille. My father's in command of the whole fleet,' he added, and you could hear he was making an effort not to sound too proud. 'But where were you last night? Here?'

Louise said they had slept in a mill and they were actually visiting Mr Heger.

'It's a long way to his house,' said Steen. 'Aren't you hungry? You could easily come home with me –

the whole house is full of people at present, so there's plenty to eat.'

Tim shook his head warningly behind Steen's back, but Louise pretended not to notice. Until Tim had had something to eat there would be no coping with him.

'Oh, thank you,' she said, 'if they won't think it too odd that Tim can't speak?'

Steen was right, there was a whole crowd of people in the house where he lived, just on the next corner. On the steps as they went in, they met a man with startlingly black hair, a Spaniard, Steen said. And a lady, who spoke Swedish, was talking to his mother. When Steen said they were hungry, Mrs Bille simply gave them a friendly smile and said, 'Tell the maid, my boy.' Then she went on talking to the Swedish lady, taking no notice of the people who were walking in and out of the house as if they lived there.

Tim ate, leaving Louise to do the talking. Steen sounded very warlike – well, that was not so strange, since his own father was the commander of the whole Danish fleet – but he was quite nice, really. A month ago, I would have been excited, too, thought Tim, with a wry smile. Only – when you found out what war meant, you didn't find it exciting at all – only ugly. But he was impressed by Louise; she did not say much, but she smiled and agreed with Steen where she could, without saying anything she didn't mean. Otherwise she just kept quiet and let him talk.

But in the end she did say, quite quietly and firmly: 'But I simply hate war, Steen. I think you should be able to talk things over, without killing people you don't even know. I really think that we would do better – oh, I don't know – to make holes in the ships' bottoms or something, so that they sink, and then nobody will have to fight and make war and burn things.'

Steen leaned forward eagerly across the table and lowered his voice. 'Of course, you can't just let things happen, but all the same, it's funny you should say that, because I heard something secret last night, when Father and Mother didn't know I was still awake; Father has had a hole bored in every ship, so that you only have to take a plug out as soon as the order is given – that might help, mightn't it, Louise?'

Louise said she was glad to know it, and soon afterwards they said goodbye.

Tim had had time to think.

The Chasseur officer had not sounded as if he believed that anything could be done. But they had carried out their errand for Uncle Arthur – there was nothing more they could do. Uncle Arthur's orders had been clear: he must get Louise out of the town before the bombardment began.

'I think we should go back to Mrs Rahbek,' he said, when Louise repeated her 'What now, Tim?' 'Perhaps she could get hold of at least one horse for us so that we can get away from the town.'

He had not much faith in this idea, and he was proved right, when Mrs Rahbek said she had no idea where to get hold of a horse, they had all been commandeered for the army. 'But you must stay with me for the time being and we'll have a talk with my cousin about what to do. We'll have to explain why you rode to Copenhagen on your own but, Tim, I think we should say you *found* that letter, or a plan or something, and could see that it was important. Your uncle might not like to have his name mixed up in this just now.'

Tim gave her a grateful smile and allowed her to run a hand through his curls. This was the right kind of aunt to have!

Louise and he slept through the rest of the day in a room that looked out on the garden. For a moment Mrs Rahbek had looked thoughtful but then she said they might as well share so that they were not taking up two rooms, in these days when one never knew if family or friends might be coming to seek refuge.

She was thinking of all that 'is it suitable' stuff, thought Louise sleepily.

In the evening they were woken by Mrs Rahbek — or Aunt Kamma, as she suggested they call her. It was quite dark, and late, too, but Uncle Drewsen had arrived and wanted to talk to them, and Mrs Rahbek thought it was time they had something to eat.

Uncle Drewsen was cheerful and did not comment on the fact that Tim was English. 'I hear from my chief today that you were heroes, too,' he said kindly. 'I didn't catch the details – we were too busy.' Then he told Aunt Kamma and Miss Christiane more about the 'Battle of Classen's Gardens', as he called it.

Suddenly he interrupted himself and smiled at Louise. 'But none of this is really fit for your ears, children,' he said. 'Aunt Kamma says you would like to get away from the town, and I'm sure Timothy's aunt must be worried about him, up there in Elsinore. And Grandfather will certainly be glad to get Louise back again – I had a message from Miss Gertrude that Louise had been so good and helpful on the day when the Eng– when the billeting began. Only I just can't think how to get you away,' he added, looking worried. 'Horses are hard to come by. But stay here for the time being, if Aunt Kamma will have you; there's no room to spare at our house. I'll see what I can do – in any case, Louise must have some decent clothes.'

It was late when they woke up again. Aunt Kamma kept them in the garden all day, explaining that she must have Louise on hand to try on the dress her aunt was making; but Tim thought to himself that it was also to keep her out of the streets. And where Louise is, I shall be too, he thought doggedly. I'm not going to move from her side, until I have her out at the Old Mill again.

Not that it was any sacrifice, because the garden was pleasant and peaceful and they were allowed to have their meals out in the summerhouse. They could see the ramparts, which rose up not far from the end of the garden, but neither of them wanted to look in that direction; they had had enough of them the day before.

Louise's uncle was stationed near the North Gate and looked in once or twice in the course of the day. He had told the aunts in Admiralsgade nothing, he said, 'so that they should not upset themselves.'

Tim saw Louise smiling a very small smile to herself.

Aunt Kamma's husband came in to breakfast from Studiegaarden, where he had been standing guard. He was a lively little red-haired gentleman – that is, he *was* a gentleman, not just any man, but you did not discover it until he spoke, and you could see the expression on his face, because his clothes were a mess, and his hair tousled, thought Tim. But how nice he was! He was so enthusiastic when they told him about the locked-up study at Hill House; and when he heard that they had read an English play to make the time pass, he sat down and talked to Tim about Shakespeare and about a new author at home, called Walter Scott. 'You must read him, my boy!' he said. 'The stories are exciting, and why shouldn't children read good books, as long as they can understand them!'

Yes, Tim decided, he liked him a lot.

But when there didn't seem to be any prospect of finding a horse the next day, either, Tim began to grow impatient. The worst moment came when Louise's uncle came in for a glass of milk.

There had been talk of some new-fangled rockets that had been invented, he said, but when General Peymann heard about them he had simply said: 'That kind of thing is not used against civilized nations!' Letters kept arriving from Lord Cathcart, saying that the general must entrust the fleet to Britain if he wanted to save Copenhagen, but General Peymann kept on saying no.

And here I sit, thought Tim, in the middle of this wretched town, with Louise, and there's not a thing I can do to stop that old idiot letting my own uncle bombard her!

Louise was remarkably uninterested, he thought. It was almost as if she had forgotten the whole thing, from the day when they handed over the letter. She helped Aunt Kamma to make a little box with a picture inside the lid, played the piano for Miss

Christiane to sing some poems that Miss Heger's fiancé had written abroad and sent home – because playing the piano was something Aunt Kamma was no good at – and most of all, she sat in the garden alone with Tim, talking, or playing dice; she taught him how to dance the minuet or showed him how to make tableaux; sometimes she picked flowers and made them up into posies which Aunt Kamma praised – but she never spoke of leaving.

On the other hand, Louise was *thinking* about it all the time, but Tim did not know that, because she did all she could to hide it.

One day, soon, when Uncle Drewsen found a horse, it would all be over. She would have to go back to the Mill and Tim would go home to his own country and she would never see him again. She would be just 'one of the children' as before, and never again belong together with anyone who knew that she was most of all Louise, and herself.

She tried to remember that Grandfather and her aunts and Uncle Drewsen were all kind enough, in their way; and all the little ones were sweet too, and it was pleasant out at the Mill by the sea.

But none of that helped, because she would never again see the glint of Tim's curly red hair somewhere up a tree, down the road or in the moonlight when she woke up in the night. Tim's brown eyes would never again look at her in the particular way that

135

showed he understood all the things no one else could ever understand.

No, Louise wished that there might be no horses in all Copenhagen; she wished that she could stay here for ever, in the sunny garden, with Tim.

Next day, towards evening, Aunt Kamma had finished the dress; it was very pretty, with little pink rosebuds printed on the material, and small puff sleeves. Aunt Christiane tied a pink ribbon in Louise's hair and said she thought Louise and Tim should go for a little walk. At first Aunt Kamma looked doubtful, but then she said, 'Oh well, all right, but you stay away from the ramparts, Tim! Perhaps you could go down and listen to the concert in King's Square – of course, children do need exercise,' she added, as if to convince herself.

The weather was lovely, and Louise and Tim easily found their way to the Raus Hotel: they knew the town quite well now, both the narrow alleyways and the broad, elegant streets and squares. Once again, there were crowds of people out walking in the fine weather, or standing listening to the music. And there was Steen Bille. 'Hallo!' he said, when he caught sight of them. Then he started, and took a closer look at Louise. 'Ah, you've got some new clothes,' he said. 'They say General Peymann's wound is inflamed and he has to stay in bed.'

Tim and Louise looked at each other. 'What

wound?' they said, both at once.

'The day before yesterday, in the attack on Classen's Gardens, he got shot in the foot because he insisted on standing up on the ramparts the whole time in readiness. My father says that he said he wished he had been hit somewhere else – the general, that is. But of course, with a wounded foot he has to stay in bed.'

Louise looked at Tim again, knowing that he also knew that the old general had meant something quite different. Someone called Steen, who waved a cheerful goodbye, and Louise told Tim in an undertone that she would never think well of the Crown Prince again! 'That poor old general – he's never served as a real soldier, Aunt Kamma says – and he has to wish himself dead just because the Crown Prince has the right to make all the decisions.'

The musicians were packing up.

'It's different at home,' said Tim. 'We have a king who's mad, too, and a Crown Prince who rules as Regent. He's not much of an ornament – though he probably never thinks of anything else – but he can't make decisions without Parliament agreeing. It's better that way: one man can't understand everything, even if he's clever. There's no certainty that your Crown Prince has fled because he's a coward – Germany is down there where he is, isn't it? And France, too, and Bonaparte.'

'Yes, but all the same!' said Louise stubbornly.

So Tim started explaining to her what a parliament was, but he had not got very far when there came a sudden, thunderous crack from all sides at once. Both of them jumped, and beside them a woman cried: 'It's started!' Everyone looked up, a streak of fire seemed to cross the sky and there was a bang, another one, and another one, until the darkening September sky was lit with the yellowish red of a firework display.

'Yes, it's started!' people round them were shouting. 'Let's get home!'

Louise stood as if glued to the spot, and Tim put his arm round her shoulders.

'We must go home too, Louise,' he said, making an effort to sound calm. 'They will be aiming at the towers in the town and the Church of Our Lady is not far from Aunt Kamma's. She may need us.'

It was easier said than done, because the alleys were crowded with women gathering their children in, firemen running round making certain the water-carts were ready, soldiers hurrying to the ramparts – and all the time bombs crashed and thundered from the reddening sky.

They had almost reached the corner of Fiol Lane when one hit the house on the opposite corner. A room lit up at once – from the inside! And they could see a woman at the window and hear her shouting:

'Oh Lord, my new curtains!'

'Stay here,' Tim ordered. 'I'll get her.'

Louise waited until he was inside the door and then ran after him.

'We need more water,' was all Tim said when he saw her.

Louise ran to get another bucketful; if they had not been so busy and if it had not been so awful, they would have been laughing, Louise thought in amazement. Because the woman in the house – Madam Pindborg was her name – was not in the least bit frightened, only outraged because those wretched Englishmen could not leave her new curtains alone! She whacked at the smouldering patches with a ladle and hauled up water and threw it about until Tim told her to use a scoop. 'We're wasting much too much water – a scoopful in the right place does more good.'

At last the fire was out and Madam Pindborg made coffee and sandwiches for them. And then another rocket fell, this time on the tablecloth.

The room was in chaos afterwards, with splintered chairs and flying fragments of cups and glasses, and the fiery sky outside to light it all up. Louise and Tim felt as if they had been hauling water for several nights already – and then Madam Pindborg broke her third ladle! 'Ugh, and all those barbs!' Tim snarled, gripping the last with his tongs and throwing it into the bucket of water.

'That was number seven,' said Madam Pindborg, sitting down on a chair that was still whole. 'Seven is my lucky number, so there won't be any more now. It would be best for you young people to go home, your parents must be worried. After all, it's – ' She looked around for the clock and laughed aloud. 'Oh, they've made short work of the clock, too! Well, well, we've come out of it alive!'

And that was true enough, thought Tim and Louise, when they were standing out in the lane again.

They were to think it many times during the next few days. After a little while it no longer seemed strange, and they had very little time to think, either, because by night they were putting out fires and by day there was plenty to do, helping all over the place.

On the first night, when they came home, Aunt Kamma had been terribly worried about them, and forbade them to go out again. In any case they were so tired and sooty and dirty that they could not resist the idea of washing and getting some sleep. But the next morning Tim took Aunt Kamma on one side and told her that they could not sit still and do nothing when there were so many people who needed help.

'It's better for Louise, too,' he insisted. 'In the end she wasn't even jumping when rockets fell last night!

When she's busy, she doesn't think so much, and I don't think she's any safer here than anywhere else, Aunt Kamma. The church tower is so terribly close.'

'Well, Tim,' Mrs Rahbek sighed and sat down, 'you're probably right. May God keep you safe, because *I* can't, in this inferno. But watch out for Louise, Tim! Keep away from the ramparts and never lose sight of her!'

Tim was thinking of the night before, when they had walked home across holes in the road, past burning houses and women dragging out their bundles, and had comforted children, and helped people who had been injured – while all the time fire fell from the red sky with the crash of thunder. It felt quite natural to say something solemn. Looking straight at Aunt Kamma, he said: 'Louise is my responsibility. I will protect her with my life, Mrs Rahbek.'

'Yes, I believe you will, Tim,' she nodded.

Louise was wearing Cousin Carl's trousers again, without anyone protesting, and they walked out into the bombed city, each with a packed lunch tied on at the waist. In the morning the bombardment had stopped and people were streaming out on to the streets, many with their goods stacked on wheelbarrows and in sacks over their shoulders, many in flight from the terrible rockets, but many more to help where they could, putting out fires, helping to bring bedclothes out into the street for the wounded, taking food up to the soldiers on the ramparts, putting out more fires, helping sick people down the ruined streets to the stables at Christiansborg, where they would be more secure behind the thick walls.

For a moment, on that first morning, Tim almost lost heart. What could they, who were only children, possibly do about all this? The grown-ups could carry bigger buckets, move heavier beams...

Then Louise said: 'We'll gather the children together, Tim. No one has time to take care of them or give them anything to eat, and they scream so dreadfully when they see someone who's been wounded.'

Her voice trembled a little, but her expression was determined, and Tim could see that she was right. It would be a real help, and it was something they could manage. They collected children from all over the place and gathered them in groups, either in Cherry Lane, or in small squares where there were no towers. Their mothers were only too glad to know that their little ones were together in comparative safety, and sometimes it was possible to find an older girl or boy who was willing to look after one bunch, and play with them.

They collected food from the Rahbek's house until Aunt Kamma had none left, and did not go home again until they were so tired that their legs were giving way under them. But it was impossible to sleep well, and before light they were out again. On Thursday they met Uncle Drewsen, red-eyed with tiredness, but in good heart. 'I must get the women and children away to Amagar,' he said. 'You go too, children – I am afraid it's not very safe in Brewer's Court.'

But Tim and Louise said they were safe enough, and in any case they were mostly out, helping other children. Uncle Drewsen bit his lip. Then he said: 'Well, yes, since I have given Aunt Kamma the responsibility I ought not to take it away from her. Tell her that Tutein's place was burned down last night.'

They met Thomas from Noah's Ark as well, on his way to Christianshavn with his mother and brothers and sisters. He waved cheerfully to them.

For a moment Tim wondered whether he ought to take Louise there too; but with all the English ships round the town – no, he was not sure it would be a good idea. In any case he thought that Louise would simply refuse to go because it was clear enough that what they were doing here was useful.

They went out every evening, until he could see that Louise was beginning to stumble with tiredness, and every time they got back to the house he felt dreadfully worried, until at last one night he woke up and decided to suggest that in future they should sleep by day instead. It was now quite obvious that the Church of Our Lady and St Peter's Church were being used as targets. So many houses in this area where their house stood had already been burned, and in any case the bombing seemed to stop in the mornings, so...

He tried to go back to sleep, but tonight things were very bad! Ugh, that one was close! He cautiously pushed back the thick curtain that Aunt Kamma had hung over the window so that no splinters could fly in.

The sky was as red as blood. 'Louise,' he whispered.

'M'mm,' she murmured sleepily.

'Louise, come out with me.'

For once she protested. 'Oh no, Tim, I'm *so* tired.'

'Louise, won't you come, please?' He hesitated, then gently stroked her hair.

'I'm coming, Tim.' He could hear that she was smiling.

Chapter Eleven

Out in the street it was as light as day – a red, unreal, evil kind of day. Bombs and rockets were whistling through the air, then came the crash, and then the shrieks of the people in the houses that had been hit. Firemen were rushing about with their axes, trying to cut the other houses free from the fire. A young woman was sitting on some steps rocking a very small baby as she sang rhythmically: 'Oh God, I can't take any more, oh God, we can't take any more.' At that moment a fireman came up with a bucket.

'Watch out!' Tim shouted, but it was too late. The bucket rolled down the street, and the man ...

Tim clasped Louise's head between his hands and turned her face against his shoulder. 'Don't look that way,' he said. 'Don't look, Louise. There is nothing we can do, he's dead. Come on, we'll go down to Mr Rahbek at the university.'

Louise followed him without speaking.

Mr Rahbek and his students were so busy that there was no more than a nod and a smile from the little red-haired gentleman. What a sight the place was!

'But up to now we've managed to put it out every time,' said one of the students, wiping the chalk dust from his forehead. 'It soon won't be worth the trouble,' said another glumly.

'Nonsense, gentlemen!' Mr Rahbek turned, his face stern. 'As long as the poor people in the streets and alleys have courage and our firemen are labouring until they drop, it is worth all our trouble!'

Tim and Louise looked at each other, thinking of the young woman. 'We can't take any more, oh God, we can't take any more,' she had chanted, probably without knowing what she was doing. But it was true. People had been so unbelievably courageous, and now they were almost finished; they had seen it for themselves on the way down here. Houses were abandoned and left to burn and there was no more water in the carts because there was no one, or too few people left to fill them. At that very moment another bomb roared through the riddled roof and blazed up in a flash.

'To the Library!' shouted Mr Rahbek.

It was high up in a loft!

'Where are we?' Louise whispered to a student.

'In the loft of Trinity Church,' he panted. 'All the

university's finest books are here.'

Mr Rahbek posted look-outs and plumped heavily down on a case. 'Shouldn't you be in bed by now, children?' he asked. 'I know how hard you work by day.' And he began to tell everyone how Louise and Tim had helped with the children so that the mothers knew they were together and in relative safety.

'We're not strong enough for the beams and the buckets of water,' said Tim, feeling awkward at this praise.

Suddenly they heard a strange, eerie and yet somehow solemn singing noise and at that moment one of the look-outs came back. 'Our Lady's Tower is in flames,' he cried. 'If it falls, then –'

'Everyone pick up books!' said Mr Rahbek forcefully. 'The fire shall not have our books! We'll break into the inner column of the Round Tower, it's hollow – Tim and Louise, help as much as you can, go slowly and don't take more than you can carry at a time. Begin here, these must be saved first.'

It was the oddest, most unreal feeling: outside, the highest tower in Copenhagen fell with a deafening crash, fires were blazing in every street, and here they were, carrying books about!

No one spoke. Louise alone whispered at regular intervals: 'Tim, remember your arm, only use it to keep the books steady.'

Mr Rahbek was ahead of them all the time, although he must be terribly tired – after all, he was practically old! But he simply went on working, selecting the books that were to go first, and then the next, and the next. 'They may take Copenhagen,' Tim heard him whisper to himself, 'but they shall not burn all the great and brilliant things that have been written: they shall not have our *books*!'

Somehow they felt they understood what he meant.

At last he declared himself satisfied, but by the time they came down the streets all around them were burning and they could hear little else but the roar of the fires and a whistling sound when another rocket crossed the sky. In a way, it was worse than when people had been screaming – now they did no more than whimper.

'Oh God, my Kamma!' cried Mr Rahbek, as he looked down North Street. And in a flash he was gone.

For a moment Tim stood there, helplessly. He had been right in dragging Louise out; at least they were still alive, but where would it be best to go now? Louise stood waiting silently beside him.

By now they did not even start when the bombs fell, and Tim never knew afterwards what had made him look up at the sound of yet another whistling descent. Then he gave Louise a tremendous shove to one side and flung himself down on her as she fell. She wriggled a little and began to cry, but Tim held on with one arm on each side of her until the crash was over and fragments were no longer falling.

Then he got up and helped her to stand. She too managed to get on her feet but went on leaning against him, crying and crying.

'Dear Louise, you mustn't cry any more now,' he said quietly. 'You are so brave! Come on, we'll go home to your grandfather now, up at the Mill.'

Louise nodded and dried her eyes on her sleeve, without noticing that the tears simply went on falling. She took Tim's hand and together they began to walk along the burning streets down towards New King's Square.

They still had not spoken a word throughout the long walk to the East Gate.

How are we going to get out? thought Tim desperately; how in the world can we escape?

But Louise went straight up to the guard without letting go of Tim's hand.

'Won't you please let us out of here?' she begged the guard, who was leaning against the wall as if that was the only thing which kept him on his feet.

He looked down at her face, its grime streaked with white by all the tears she had shed. Without a word he unlocked the gate and opened it just wide enough – and they were outside.

Tim smiled at her. 'You managed that splendidly,' he said, straightening his clothes a little. 'Come on, we'll go down to Classen's Gardens and rest for a bit. It's quite quiet down there.'

They sat down behind the bush where they had been before and were silent for a time.

Then Louise said, wonderingly: 'Are a few ships worth that, Tim? All those dead people, all those burned houses, all that horror?'

'No. Yes. Louise, I don't know ... but people have to defend themselves. Uncle Arthur said what would happen, do you remember? That bit about one man not getting power over all the others. I don't know. I don't think we should speculate too much about it. Perhaps we can do something about it when we're grown up.'

'I shall never be grown up enough to believe people should turn the sky red with fire and blood, no matter what,' said Louise.

And then, astonishingly, she fell asleep!

It was almost light now; Tim sat looking down at her face, so small and white under the soot and dirt, the dark-brown lashes curling outwards a little, like tiny fans. She was muttering something in her sleep and scratching at the grass with one hand. Tim took off his jacket, rolled it up and slipped it cautiously under her head as a pillow.

He must get hold of a horse. Somehow or other, he

must get hold of a horse which could carry her home to her grandfather. She was far too tired to endure any more.

He rose silently and pulled a handkerchief out of his pocket – an almost clean one that he had got from Mrs Rahbek the day before and forgotten about. Then he cut a branch off a bush, tied the handkerchief to it and walked slowly, but with a very straight back, down towards the spot where his uncle had shouted out an order, so few days ago.

The man on guard had seen him and was watching him approach, when there came a scream from behind him.

'No, Tim! He'll shoot you – Tim – oh no – Tim!'

Tim clenched his teeth. Of course nobody would shoot a person coming with a white flag – and only a boy at that!

Louise reached the guard at the same time as Tim.

'Are you stark-staring mad, children!' cried the man, furious. 'What if I had shot first and taken a closer look afterwards?'

Tim did not answer. It had taken all he had left to force himself to walk down to the English position, hoping that the guard would look before he shot.

Now another man came up, an officer, as they could see from his collar.

'What the hell is all this row about?' he said

angrily. 'But – ' he looked more closely at Tim
' – isn't that a Brandon? There's no mistaking
that colour!'

'I am Tim Brandon, sir,' said Tim. 'My uncle was
here the other day – my Uncle Arthur – I heard his
voice. My friend Louise is very tired and I want to
take her home to her grandfather, but it's such a long
way, I – ' At that point his voice almost broke,
dammit! Tim swallowed furiously and went on: 'I
thought perhaps we could borrow a horse, it's
impossible to get hold of one in the city.'

'You've come from inside the city?' said the
officer, startled.

'Yes,' said Louise. 'We had an errand there. It
didn't work out ... now all the streets are burning,
and the dead children and people – there were none
left to help.'

She sounded all wrong, thought Tim anxiously,
taking her hand: sort of indifferent, somehow.

'Come inside, children,' said the officer. 'You need
a cup of hot soup and a bit of a wash, as far as I can
see. Meanwhile, I'll see what we can do.'

He put an arm round each of them and Tim saw
that his hands were shaking a little. His face was
terribly stern, but he wasn't angry with them any
more, Tim thought with relief.

The soup was good and beautifully hot, and there
were cheese sandwiches too. 'Eat up now, Tim,' said

152

Louise again, and Tim ate, partly because it was so good to hear her saying something quite ordinary. She herself did not eat anything, but she drank her soup.

The officer left them to eat and drink in peace; then he made a sign to Tim and took him a little to one side. 'It's only shock, Tim, she'll soon be all right again. I popped a tiny bit of soothing medicine in her soup. You could rest here, of course, but I think you're right that it would be better to get far away from the city as quickly as possible. What's up with your arm?'

Tim said, oh, that had been a long time ago, just a bullet that had gone straight through. Then he remembered something. 'But if you see Colonel Sheridan out at Hill House, will you apologise for us. You see we *had* to run away?'

The officer smiled a little and promised. 'And what shall I tell your uncle, Tim?'

'Tell him – ' Tim blinked once or twice ' – tell him that – that we were in time, but it didn't help. And tell him I simply could not get Louise out before the bombs came, but we have been together all the time. Tell him she's been so very, very brave, tell him nothing has happened to her ...'

Then his voice failed him. 'Say that I'm sorry.'

He realized with shame that blinking his eyes had not helped, one or two tears had managed to spill

153

over. Fortunately the officer happened to be looking the other way. Then he said that in his opinion it looked as if, on the contrary, Tim had done everything he should and a little more, 'and your little friend too. Ride away now, Tim, and do your very best to forget what you've seen these last few days – but don't forget each other! That will at least be some gain from this whole wretched story.'

'Louise is not someone you forget,' said Tim simply.

The air was fresh and beautiful and now smelled of nothing but air. The sky before them was blue, as they had almost forgotten it could be, and the sun shone, laying broad streaks of silver across the light blue Sound so that it glittered and almost hurt their eyes. Tim and Louise rode right down to the sandy wheeltracks along the beach and up there by the big oak trees was the place where they had turned inland, all that time ago.

They did not talk much; Louise took care to seem happy and normal, but it was never any good trying to fool Tim.

'Is something wrong, Louise?' he said suddenly, stopping the horse.

Louise, who was sitting in front of him, shook her

head, but she did not turn, so her curls simply tickled his nose.

'That tickles! Turn round!'

Louise shook her head again.

'Louise, we shall forget about all this, almost – if we try hard. We did what we could, didn't we? You can't do more than that. And – we've got each other, haven't we?'

'Not for long now. You'll be sent home, of course, and –'

She was taking great care with her voice, but now something wet was dripping on to Tim's hand.

'Louise, of course I shall be sent home soon, and so will you. Turn round, you idiot!' He took hold of her head. 'Just as I thought – you know I don't like it when you cry! What on earth has that got to do with anything, our being sent home? We'll be grown up later on, shan't we, and then we can get married.'

Louise felt everything begin to spin round: the sky, the sun, everything. 'Do you want that, Tim?'

'Well, not now, of course. We'll have to be grown up first. Do girls have to be so silly? Who else could I marry, for Heaven's sake!'

To be with Tim for always, to know that as soon as they grew up Tim would be there, always ... Louise dried her face on his sleeve and smiled.

'Then I'm not sad any more,' she said joyously. 'It

155

was only, because—'

Tim smiled back with delight. 'Because you're so silly, right?'

Also by Anne Holm

THE HOSTAGE

Christopher, the son of the Danish Prime Minister, is kidnapped by Mr Moller, one of his father's political opponents. When the operation is taken over by the Red Brigade, who capture Moller's son as well, the kidnapping goes badly wrong, and Chris soon realises that, to stay alive, they must both escape . . .

Anne Holm

I AM DAVID

'David lay quite still in the darkness of the camp, waiting for the signal.

"You must get away tonight," the man had told him. "Stay awake so that you're ready just before the guard is changed. When you see me strike a match, the current will be cut off and you can climb over – you'll have half a minute for it, no more."'

Silent and watchful, David, the boy from the camp, tramps across Europe, knowing that at any moment *they* may catch up with him.

'. . . the boy's strange intense, self-preserving view of life is realised superbly.'   *The Sunday Times*

'A most compassionate, powerful, moving book, full of hope and tenderness.'   *The Evening Standard*

A Selected List of Fiction from Mammoth

While every effort is made to keep prices low, it is sometimes necessary to increase prices at short notice. Mandarin Paperbacks reserves the right to show new retail prices on covers which may differ from those previously advertised in the text or elsewhere.

The prices shown below were correct at the time of going to press.

☐	7497 0978 2	**Trial of Anna Cotman**	Vivien Alcock	£2.50
☐	7497 0712 7	**Under the Enchanter**	Nina Beachcroft	£2.50
☐	7497 0106 4	**Rescuing Gloria**	Gillian Cross	£2.50
☐	7497 0035 1	**The Animals of Farthing Wood**	Colin Dann	£3.50
☐	7497 0613 9	**The Cuckoo Plant**	Adam Ford	£3.50
☐	7497 0443 8	**Fast From the Gate**	Michael Hardcastle	£1.99
☐	7497 0136 6	**I Am David**	Anne Holm	£2.99
☐	7497 0295 8	**First Term**	Mary Hooper	£2.99
☐	7497 0033 5	**Lives of Christopher Chant**	Diana Wynne Jones	£2.99
☐	7497 0601 5	**The Revenge of Samuel Stokes**	Penelope Lively	£2.99
☐	7497 0344 X	**The Haunting**	Margaret Mahy	£2.99
☐	7497 0537 X	**Why The Whales Came**	Michael Morpurgo	£2.99
☐	7497 0831 X	**The Snow Spider**	Jenny Nimmo	£2.99
☐	7497 0992 P	**My Friend Flicka**	Mary O'Hara	£2.99
☐	7497 0525 6	**The Message**	Judith O'Neill	£2.99
☐	7497 0410 1	**Space Demons**	Gillian Rubinstein	£2.50
☐	7497 0151 X	**The Flawed Glass**	Ian Strachan	£2.99

All these books are available at your bookshop or newsagent, or can be ordered direct from the publisher. Just tick the titles you want and fill in the form below.

Mandarin Paperbacks, Cash Sales Department, PO Box 11, Falmouth, Cornwall TR10 9EN.

Please send cheque or postal order, no currency, for purchase price quoted and allow the following for postage and packing:

UK including BFPO   £1.00 for the first book, 50p for the second and 30p for each additional book ordered to a maximum charge of £3.00.

Overseas including Eire   £2 for the first book, £1.00 for the second and 50p for each additional book thereafter.

NAME (Block letters) ....

ADDRESS ....

....

☐ I enclose my remittance for ....

☐ I wish to pay by Access/Visa Card Number

Expiry Date